LEE ALEXANDER

The Fortuitous Few

A Chronicle of Courage

SHADOW PAGES
PRESS

First published by Shadow Pages Press, LLC 2024

This novel is entirely a work of fiction. The names, characters and incidents portrayed in it are the work of the author's imagination. Any resemblance to actual persons, living or dead, events or localities is entirely coincidental.

Library of Congress Control Number: Pending

Title: The Fortuitous Few: A Chronicle of Courage

Author: Lee Alexander

Digital Disstribution | 2024

Paperback |2024

First edition

ISBN: 979-8-9911360-8-2

This book is for all the members of our D&D party. These characters are tours. I provided the story line and you gave them and the story life. Thank you for the hours of laughs and good times. Thought the Nat 1's rolled, it is always a Nat 20 good time.

Chapter 1

Rashe, the charismatic drakonisk bard with scales shimmering in vibrant hues, and his loyal companion Adran, a vigilant wood elf monk, bodyguard, and long-time friend, arrived in the bustling city of Kelrabith. Their journey had been long and filled with anticipation, leading them to this vibrant metropolis that teemed with opportunities waiting to be seized. Together, they sought respite from the road and a chance to forge their destinies in the vibrant tapestry of Kelrabith.

Rashe was a captivating sight to behold, a creature of mythical allure and musical prowess. As he moves through the world, his golden scales catch the light like a thousand stars, and the enchanting aura he emits leaves all who encounter him spellbound and captivated by the magic he carries within. Rashe stands tall, a mesmerizing blend of dragon and humanoid, a creature known as a golden drakonisk. His lithe and graceful frame exudes both power and elegance, evident in every stride he takes. Rashe's skin was adorned with shining scales, each shimmering in vibrant hues that seemed to dance in the changing light. The scales, reminiscent of molten gold, cascade across his body like a treasure hoard, catching every ray of sunlight and radiating an otherworldly glow. His striking, angular features are a delicate balance of human and dragon attributes. He possesses expressive almond-shaped eyes that glimmer with a pearl of inner wisdom and mischief, their color a mesmerizing mix of fiery red and molten gold. Above those captivating orbs, his sleek and elongated brows give him an alluring and intense gaze.

Rashe's attire was as bewitching as his appearance. He dons a tunic crafted from fine silk, interwoven with golden threads, which cascades down his willowy. The garment was adorned with delicate patterns of dragon scales, a nod to his ancestral heritage. Golden filigree ornaments embellish the edges of the tunic, shimmering like the glint of sun-kissed rivers. Around his waist, Rashe wears a belt fashioned from a supple leather dyed in a deep crimson, the color reminiscent of smoldering embers. Hanging from it, he keeps an assortment of finely crafted pouches, each containing mysterious tokens, spell components, and small musical instruments that aid in his performances. On his feet, Rashe wears soft, supple boots made from the hide of a mythical creature, which provide silent and agile movements as he gracefully navigates the world around him.

Adran, the vigilant wood elf monk, embodies the harmony of the wilderness, standing tall and poised with an aura of quiet strength and swift agility. His verdant eyes gleam with unwavering determination, ready to protect those under his care. With finely chiseled features and slightly pointed ears attuned to nature's sounds, Adran's warm earth-toned skin was adorned with delicate patterns, a testament to his wood elf heritage and connection with the ancient forest spirits.

His practical yet elegant attire blends effortlessly with the foliage, making him an elusive protector. A finely crafted tunic in deep greens and browns allows him to blend with the surroundings, while a leather belt adorned with pouches and small satchels holds essential herbs, potions, and tools for his bodyguard duties. Hanging from the belt, wooden beads and charms produced a soft jingling, which served as a gentle warning. His finely honed wooden staff, intricately carved with nature-inspired patterns, becomes an extension of the vigilant wood elf himself.

Clad in supple leather boots in mossy greens and earthy tones, Adran moves effortlessly through the underbrush. As a guardian of the ancient forest and those seeking shelter, he exudes tranquility and readiness to respond swiftly to any danger. Adran, the vigilant wood elf monk, and bodyguard, was a testament to the timeless beauty and mystery of the woodland itself.

Guided by the whispers of fate, Rashe and Adran found themselves drawn to the renowned Grand Griffon Tavern that stood at the heart of Kelrabith like a majestic beacon, its exterior adorned with intricately carved wooden beams that seemed to come alive in the flickering torchlight. As Rashe and Adran crossed its threshold, the atmosphere within shifted instantly, embracing them in a symphony of sensations.

The scent of spiced ale and savory meats mingled with the warm fragrance of polished oak and freshly cut flowers, creating an intoxicating aroma that teased the senses. The tavern's dimly lit interior glowed with a golden hue, cast by the myriad of candles that danced on every surface, flickering like stars in the night sky.

The air was alive with the enchanting melodies of a skilled bard, whose fingers danced gracefully across the strings of a lute, weaving a tapestry of sound that resonated within the hearts of the patrons. Each note seemed to caress the soul, conjuring memories of distant lands and forgotten loves.

Yet, amidst the captivating music, all eyes were drawn to Rashe, the charismatic drakonisk bard. His scales shimmered in vibrant hues, reflecting the light like precious gems. The very essence of the tavern responded to his presence as if the wooden beams whispered secrets and the candles leaned closer to bask in his glow.

A vibrant aura surrounded Rashe, drawing curious onlookers like moths to a flame. The allure of his magic was undeniable, and the patrons couldn't help but be enchanted by his presence. They leaned in, captivated by his every movement, eager to experience the spell that seemed to radiate from his very being.

The tavern hummed with a sense of anticipation, as if the air crackled with energy, waiting for the next verse of the bard's song. The patrons leaned in, their hearts open like books, ready to be filled with the enchanting tale he wove. Even the shadows seemed to retreat, unable to resist the allure of Rashe's vibrant presence.

The Grand Griffon Tavern had earned its reputation as a place where dreams took flight, and destinies were forever altered. It was a sanctuary for those seeking respite from the troubles of the world, and a haven for the lost souls searching for purpose. Within its walls, the lines between reality and fantasy blurred, and the mundane gave way to the extraordinary.

As Rashe and Adran found their place among the patrons, they became part of the tavern's living tapestry, adding their own vibrant threads to the stories that unfolded within its walls. The Grand Griffon Tavern embraced them like an old friend, welcoming them into its warm embrace, ready to guide them on their journey through the vibrant tapestry of Kelrabith.

Adran, ever vigilant and watchful, ensured their safety within the lively tavern. His keen senses, honed through years of experience, scanned the surroundings, his gaze sweeping across the sea of faces. With a subtle nod, he reassured Rashe that they were in a place of both respite and opportunity, ready to navigate the currents of this city and embrace the myriad adventures that awaited them.

Meanwhile, after days of traversing treacher-ous roads and wearying nights, Morros, a skilled and nimble-fingered Tiefling, arrived in Kelrabith. With his coin purse growing lighter with each passing day, he yearned for a suitable place to ply his talents and secure the funds necessary to sustain his journey. As he navigated the bustling streets, his eyes, sharp and perceptive, scanned the surroundings, seeking that one opportune moment to exercise his agile dexterity. But Morros had aspirations beyond mere thievery; he longed for legitimate work that would harness his unique skills and offer a chance at a brighter future. Determined and resourceful, he embraced the vibrant city, ready to seize every opportunity that lay before him.

And so, it was within the heart of Kelrabith that the Grand Griffon Tavern beckoned to Morros. Its lively ambiance, brimming with energy and potential, whispered promises of both wealth and notoriety. It was here, amidst the raucous laughter and clinking of glasses, that Morros believed he could find the means to not only replenish his dwindling coin purse but also lay the groundwork for a life beyond the shadows.

However, unbeknownst to Rashe, Adran, and Morros, on the other side of town, Jalaris Bearsden and Averill Kelrabith sat at a corner table within the dimly lit Grindle Tavern. Their conversation carried the weight of a carefully crafted contract, for they were finalizing plans to secure a rare and coveted book. Jalaris, known for his prowess as an intermediary, had undertaken the responsibility of assembling a team and supplying the necessary goods and provisions to ensure the success of their mission. Averill, the book's rightful owner, eagerly awaited its safe return, ready to provide a generous reward upon its retrieval.

With arrangements made, each man set off on his own path. Jalaris, driven by his sense of duty, rode to another tavern across town, his steed fastened outside, as he sought suitable candidates for the daunting task at hand. The Grand Griffon Tavern beckoned, its vibrant aura drawing him in, as he crossed its threshold, ready to weave the threads of fate and destiny together in pursuit of their shared objective.

Little did they know that the paths of Rashe, Adran, Morros, and Jalaris were on a collision course, bound to intersect within the lively embrace of the Grand Griffon Tavern. There, amidst the melodic strains of Rashe's bardic talents, the nimble fingers of Morros, and the watchful gaze of Adran, their lives would converge, setting them on a course filled with challenges, discovery, and the untamed allure of both fortune and fate. The stage was set, and the tapestry of their intertwined destinies awaited its first stroke in the bustling city of Kelrabith.

Chapter 2

Rashe had secured employment at The Grand Griffon Tavern for the next ten days. With the exceptionally large tavern full of patrons Rashe skillfully crafted his improvisations, patrons joyfully chatted and sipped their drinks in sync with the beat. His mesmerizing charisma and performance captivated everyone present, weaving an atmosphere of liveliness and harmony with each melodious flourish.The mysterious and captivating tunes from the instrument radiated a certain otherworldly charm, compelling even the most jaded drinkers to marvel at its beguiling poignancy. As the patrons relished the music, they felt compelled to approach the stage and deposit gratuities of coins in an open purse that he had placed at the stage's boundary. The tavern keeper paid Rashe a meager wage, a room, a bath, and food, but not drink. All of which he shared with Adran. The gratuities helped pay for drinks and provisions for their next excursion.

Adran sat amongst the throng of patrons and kept a vigilant watch on them. He'd been in this line of work long enough to have seen it all, and he could anticipate any possible danger before it presented itself. His years of experience and monkish dexterity gave him an advantage that allowed him to size up a crowd almost instantly and assess potential threats swiftly and methodically. His demeanor was relaxed but resolute; there was no mistaking his confidence as he surveyed the area with expert precision. However, he always maintained a reasonable distance not to distract those compelled to come up and tip Rashe.

In the crowd sat Morros, a Tiefling passing through the coast, looking for work that suited his particular talents. He was seated at a booth that was out of the way but close to where groups of patrons would walk by as they went to get more drinks from the bar. Morros had come in with only a few coins in his purse and ordered a fine meal and ale. After his order had been delivered, he paid the waitress, and now he was down to his last few coins. A band of inebriated humans supported each other as they swayed and stumbled from the bar to the door. They exhibited a wry camaraderie borne of long hours spent guzzling alcohol and sharing stories. A nonpareil sense of familiarity lingered between them as they jested each other. As they clumsily groped their way toward the exit, they stumbled over Morros' foot which was conveniently in their way. As the intoxicated band of friends helped each other up, Morros aided them and used his keen skills to remove their purses. With the commotion in the tavern, it was easy not to be observed by anyone except for the local contract intermediary. Jalaris always has an eye out for new talent.

Jalaris stood up and ambled over to the booth that Morros was occupying. He slowly sat across from him, smiled, and said, "you are very good at sleight of hand."

Morros watched as he sat, listened to what Jalaris said, and replied, "I am sure I do not know what you are referring to."

"Of course not, and please know that I am looking for talented individuals to take some contract work, not blackmail or turn you over to the city guard." Chuckled Jalaris.

Morros flagged down the waitress and said, "what would you like to drink while we discuss the contract you have in mind."

Jalaris looked at the waitress and said, "Talisa, please bring one of my opulent wines and two glasses." He looked back at Morros and continued, "I have a reserve of fine wine just for occasions like this."

As Talisa walked off to get the wine, Jalaris

introduced himself to Morros. He told Morros that he was one of the contract intermediaries in town and that most of his contracts came from a more affluent clientele than other intermediaries. These contracts have high rewards for those fortunate enough to be employed with them. Talisa returned and placed a bottle of wine and two glasses on the table. Jalaris set a gold piece on her tray as she turned to walk away. Jalaris resumed talking about his contracts and himself as he poured each of them a glass of wine. Before discussing the contract details that he wanted to employ Morros, he asked about his background and abilities, even though the sleight of hand and attention to detail he had observed told him almost all he needed to know.

Morros listened intently to Jalaris, his curiosity piqued by the prospect of lucrative contracts and the opportunity to put his skills to good use. As he sipped the wine, he considered his response, careful not to reveal too much about his past.

"Well, Jalaris, I come from a varied background," Morros began, his voice steady and measured. "I have honed my skill in the art of stealth, agility, and precision. You've already witnessed my abilities with sleight of hand, and I can assure you that my attention to detail was unparalleled."

He paused for a moment, gathering his thoughts before continuing. "I have traversed these lands as a wanderer, always seeking new challenges and opportunities. I am adept at infiltration, reconnaissance, and, if need be, removing obstacles quietly and swiftly. My Tiefling heritage grants me certain advantages in the shadows, and I have learned to use them to my advantage."

Morros took another sip of the wine, savoring its rich flavor, before meeting Jalaris' gaze. "But I must ask, what kind of contract are we discussing here? What is it that you require my particular set of skills for?"

Jalaris leaned back in his chair, swirling the wine in his glass thoughtfully. "Ah, excellent questions, my friend," he replied, a glimmer of excitement dancing in his eyes. "The contract I have in mind involves the recovery of a unique book. Its contents are said to hold ancient knowledge and untapped power, and its current owner is willing to pay handsomely for its safe return." He leaned forward, lowering his voice slightly to add a touch of intrigue. "The task won't be without its challenges, of course. There will be dangers to navigate, traps to overcome, and potentially competing factions seeking the book for their own purposes. But the rewards, both in terms of gold and the knowledge within those pages, are well worth the risks."

Morros nodded, his interest solidifying. "I am intrigued by the prospect, Jalaris. The recovery of such a valuable artifact aligns well with my skills and aspirations. Please, tell me more about the specifics of this contract."

Jalaris smiled, pleased with Morros' response. He began to unfold the details of the contract, describing the location where the book was last seen, the obstacles they might face, and the timeline for completion. He emphasized the need for discretion, caution, and the importance of working as a team to achieve success.

As they delved deeper into the contract, their conversation ebbed and flowed, the wine continuing to flow as they discussed strategies, potential rewards, and the nature of the enigmatic employer who sought the book's return. And as the night wore on, Morros found himself drawn in by the allure of the contract, its promises of adventure, and the opportunity to test his skills in a meaningful endeavor. He couldn't help but feel a sense of excitement building within him as he contemplated the possibilities.

Finally, after hours of discussion, Jalaris reached the conclusion. "So, Morros, what do you say? Will you join me in this venture? Will you lend your talents to the recovery of the unique book?"

Morros raised his glass, a glimmer of determination in his eyes. "I accept your offer, Jalaris. Let us embark on this journey together and secure that book for our enigmatic employer."

Jalaris grinned, a mixture of relief and excitement evident on his face. "Excellent! Tomorrow morning, we shall gather the rest of our team and you shall set off on your quest. Rest well tonight, Morros, for tomorrow marks the beginning of a grand adventure." As they clinked their glasses together, sealing their agreement, Morros couldn't help but feel a surge of anticipation. He knew that the path ahead would be treacherous, but the promise of both gold and knowledge beckoned him, igniting a fire within his soul. The stage was set, and the journey awaited them in the morning.

With renewed purpose, Morros savored the last sip of wine, his mind already buzzing with plans and possibilities. As he bid Jalaris farewell for the night and made his way to his lodgings, he couldn't help but feel a sense of destiny unfolding. The Grand Griffon Tavern, once just a stop along his journey, had now become the catalyst for a daring undertaking that would test his mettle and shape his future. As he closed his eyes, his thoughts filled with visions of hidden chambers, ancient tomes, and the thrill of outwitting formidable adversaries. The anticipation of the coming dawn infused him with a surge of determination, knowing that the journey ahead would forge him into something greater than he had ever been before. And so, with the weight of possibility on his shoulders, Morros drifted into a restless sleep, eager to embark on the path that lay before him, guided by the call of adventure and the promise of riches untold.

Chapter 3

In the morning, Morros returned to the Grand Griffin to meet with Jalaris. As he stepped through the entrance, Morros immediately noticed Jalaris, who was already seated at a sturdy wooden table. However, what caught his attention were the two individuals accompanying him. To his left sat Rashe, a captivating drakonisk whose enchanting melodies had filled the tavern the previous night. To his right was a domineer and graceful wood elf, exuding an aura of unwavering loyalty and a strong sense of protection. Morros couldn't help but recall how the wood elf slipped through the crowd almost unnoticed ensuring the safety of Rashe, making it unmistakable that he was there for his protection. His movements and attention had left an indelible impression on him. Feeling a sense of familiarity, he approached the table with a purposeful stride, taking the last empty seat and joining this intriguing group of adventurers. Little did they know that their destinies were about to intertwine in ways they could never have imagined.

As Morros settled into his seat, Jalaris greeted him with a warm smile. "Ah, Morros, I'm glad you could join us," he said, his voice filled with anticipation. "Allow me to introduce the rest of our team. This is Rashe," he gestured to the drakonisk bard seated to his left.

Rashe offered a friendly nod, his vibrant scales shimmering in the morning light. "Greetings, Morros," he greeted, his voice melodious and infused with a natural charm. "I heard about your impressive sleight of hand skills last night. I believe we'll make a formidable team."

Morros returned the nod, already feeling a sense of camaraderie with Rashe. "Likewise, Rashe. I can see that we share a passion for our respective crafts. I'm excited to see what we can achieve together."

Jalaris, sitting at the table alongside them, listened intently as the introductions unfolded. He wore an expression of anticipation, his role primarily that of an information giver and facilitator for the group's mission.

"Indeed, the two of you possess exceptional skills," Jalaris chimed in. "Morros, your expertise in stealth and sleight of hand, and Rashe, your enchanting melodies and bardic magic, will be instrumental in our mission."

At that moment Rashe introduced Adran, a close

friend and loyal companion of his. He was seated to the right of Jalaris where he could have an unhindered view of the door and others that were in the tavern. His presence emanates a calm and steady demeanor, but his eyes darted from movement to movement showing his innate ability to strike or defend with ferocity when needed.

Adran nodded towards Morros, acknowledging his presence. "Greetings, Morros," he said with a warm smile. "Jalaris has spoken highly of your abilities. I'm glad to have you join our team."

Morros returned the greeting with a nod, appreciating Adran's friendly demeanor. "Thank you, Adran. It's a pleasure to meet you. I've observed your skills and know that we'll make a formidable group."

Rashe, the drakonisk bard, chimed in, his eyes filled with excitement. "Indeed! Adran and I have been friends for a long time. He was a skilled warrior and a loyal friend. Having him by our side will give us an extra layer of protection and support."

Jalaris interjected, his voice filled with confidence. "Wonderful! With your combined skills and camaraderie, we have a strong foundation for our mission. Now, let me provide you with the crucial details."

Morros and Rashe leaned in, their focus shifting

entirely towards Jalaris as he began to unveil the specifics of their mission. Adran listened intently as he continued to keep a skillful eye on the surroundings. Jalaris explained that the Codex of Whispers was hidden inside the home of a powerful cult leader. The house was heavily protected with traps, intricate protection spells, and a dedicated group of cult followers guarding it.

"The cult leader was a formidable individual," Jalaris warned. "He possesses great knowledge and power, and he won't easily part with the Codex. It will require careful planning, teamwork, and resourcefulness to retrieve it."

Morros studied the map and listened attentively as Jalaris described the various challenges they would face. He couldn't help but feel a mixture of excitement and caution, realizing the gravity of their mission. Morros being the skilled rogue was memorizing the map and developing an entrance plan in his mind along with not less than three escape routes in case things went unfavorably.

Rashe's eyes sparkled with determination. "We shall overcome these obstacles," he declared, his voice filled with unwavering confidence. "With Morros' stealth and sleight of hand, Adran's strength and combat skills, and my bardic magic, we will navigate the traps, dismantle the protection spells, and face the cult followers head-on."

Jalaris nodded, impressed by the group's resolve. "Indeed, your unique skills will be essential in this mission. Remember to use your talents wisely and work together. The Codex of Whispers holds immense power, and we must ensure its recovery and return it to the rightful owner so it was no longer in the wrong hands."

With their plans starting to take shape, the group continued their discussion, strategizing ways to approach the cult leader's home, counter the traps and spells, and overcome the cult followers. They were aware that danger awaited them, but their determination remained steadfast. Jalaris, as the information giver and facilitator, provided the necessary resources, guidance, and support from the outside. Although he wouldn't physically join the adventure, his role was crucial in ensuring the team had the information and assistance they needed.

"Remember, timing and coordination will be key," Jalaris reminded them. "Take advantage of any opportunities that arise, and rely on each other's strengths. Together, you have the potential to retrieve the Codex of Whispers."

With their plans finalized, the group gathered their gear and prepared to face the challenges that awaited them in the cult leader's home. The air was filled with a mixture of determination and anticipation as they set off on their mission, knowing that they would need to rely on their skills, teamwork, and resourcefulness to succeed. Knowing that The Codex of Whispers held ancient secrets and immense power, the group was determined to protect it from remaining in the wrong hands. The journey ahead would be fraught with danger, but united as a team, they were ready to face whatever awaited them and bring the precious artifact back to safety.

Chapter 4

In the mystical realm of Exiorea, a foreboding darkness cast its shadow over the land as the sinister Baatorian cult rose to prominence, their intentions veiled in malevolence. Whispers among sages and adventurers spoke of the Codex of Whispers, a legendary tome said to contain ancient secrets and immense power, hidden deep within the cult leader's mansion. Comprising a valiant and diverse party, the adventurers Rashe, the eloquent bard with a mesmerizing voice; Adran, the agile and disciplined monk adept at the martial arts; and Morros, the cunning and stealthy rogue assassin, were contracted to retrieve the Codex and safeguard the realm from impending doom.

Through a network of informants, the party discovered that the cult leader was hosting a grand ball at the mansion. A perfect opportunity presented itself – the guise of attendees would allow them to infiltrate the mansion undetected. However, attending the ball meant the party had to meticulously plan their strategy and appearances. Rashe, with their enchanting music and eloquence, would pose as a renowned performer, while Adran and Morros would assume the roles of esteemed guests, their skills as a monk and rogue enabling them to blend seamlessly into the company.

As rumors of a grand ball to be held at the Baatorian cult leader's mansion reached their ears, Rashe, Adran, and Morros saw this as the opportune moment to infiltrate the secretive stronghold and uncover the whereabouts of the elusive Codex of Whispers. With determination in their hearts, they devised a clever plan to pose as guests at the extravagant affair.

Step 1: Gathering Intelligence

Before attending the ball, the party spent several days gathering crucial information. Rashe's silver tongue and charismatic presence allowed them to blend seamlessly into high society, attending various social gatherings and engaging in casual conversations to glean details about the mansion's layout, security, and the notable guests expected at the ball. Adran used his mastery of stealth to eavesdrop on conversations and observe the guards' routines, while Morros used his espionage skills to acquire the appropriate attire and forged invitations.

Step 2: Creating New Identities

As the date of the ball approached, the party transformed themselves into new identities, adopting personas that would allow them to blend in with the cultured and sophisticated guests. Rashe assumed the identity of a renowned performer from a distant land, with a captivating voice that had enchanted crowds across the realm. Adran presented himself as a prestigious and enigmatic foreign dignitary, his elegant demeanor and fluid movements attracting curiosity and intrigue. Morros, skilled in disguise, adopted the guise of a wealthy noble's elusive and mysterious cousin, rumored to have a taste for danger and excitement.

Step 3: Acquiring Invitations

With forged invitations in hand, the party confidently approached the mansion's entrance on the night of the ball. As they passed through the grand gates, the subtle sway of Rashe's cloak and the confidence exuding from Adran and Morros helped them sail through the scrutiny of the guards.

Step 4: Engaging with the Guests

Once inside, Rashe took center stage, captivating the attendees with enchanting melodies and entrancing performances. Their music became a thread that wove the party into the fabric of the event, drawing attention away from their true purpose. Adran and Morros mingled effortlessly, strategically engaging in conversations with notable guests and influential members of the cult, all the while subtly gathering information and observing their surroundings.

Step 5: Posing as Entertainers

During a brief intermission, the party used their diverse skills to participate in an improvised performance. Adran demonstrated a mesmerizing display of martial arts, displaying the grace and skill of a true master, while Morros engaged in a thrilling acrobatic act, leaving the crowd awestruck. Rashe skillfully intertwined their music with the performances, enhancing the spectacle and further solidifying their identities as esteemed entertainers.

Step 6: Keeping a Low Profile

As the night progressed, the party remained vigilant, avoiding drawing undue attention to their true intentions. While Rashe's enchanting presence kept the focus on their performances, Adran and Morros covertly scouted for hidden passages and clues to the Codex's location, all without raising suspicion.

With their plan executed to perfection, Rashe,

Adran, and Morros seamlessly infiltrated the Baatorian cult leader's mansion, hidden in plain sight as guests of the illustrious ball. The time had come to uncover the mysteries that lay within the mansion's shadowy depths and bring the Codex of Whispers out of obscurity and into the light.

Inside, the party encountered a series of challenges, testing their ingenuity and resourcefulness. In the main library, they discovered cult followers diligently guarding key information, and after a clever ruse, they managed to locate clues to the Codex's whereabouts – hidden in a secret magic portal concealed within a sarcophagus in the mansion's basement.

The air crackled with tension as the adventure party, Rashe the bard, Adran the monk, and Morros the rogue assassin, stood face to face with the dreaded chain demon. Towering over them, the demon's massive iron chains writhed like serpents, its malevolence evident in its fiery eyes. The stench of sulfur and brimstone filled the air, as if the very essence of darkness had taken form.

With a roar that shook the ground beneath their feet, the chain demon lunged forward, its massive chains swinging wildly towards the party. Rashe's heart pounded, but the bard's voice did not falter as they unleashed an inspiring melody, filling their companions with newfound courage. Adran moved with unmatched grace, dodging the demon's attacks with nimble footwork, while Morros vanished into the shadows, reappearing behind the beast to land a precise strike with deadly precision.

The demon's chains clanged against Morros' blade, sending sparks flying through the air. Adran's fists blurred into a flurry of strikes, connecting with the demons armored hide. Rashe weaved enchanting spells into their songs, compelling the demon to momentarily hesitate. But the chain demon was relentless, its iron chains lashing out like vengeful tendrils, threatening to overwhelm the adventurers.

Gritting their teeth, the party fought on, and each member drawing strength from the others. Rashe's music echoed through the battlefield, inspiring their allies to push forward with renewed determination. Adran's monk training allowed them to tap into their inner ki, channeling it into devastating strikes that cracked the demon's armor. Morros danced between the demon's chains, inflicting deep wounds with every opportune opening.

As the battle raged on, the chain demon grew more ferocious, its attacks intensifying with unholy fury. But the adventurers remained undaunted, united in their cause to protect the realm from this malevolent creature. Rashe's haunting melodies became a symphony of bravery, uplifting the party as they fought as one.

Finally, with a concerted effort, the party managed to weaken the chain demon, its iron chains falling limply to the ground. Seizing the moment, Adran delivered a decisive blow, striking true to the demon's heart. As the beast let out a haunting howl, its form dissipated into shadows, vanishing from the realm.

Breathing heavily, the adventurers stood victorious, their clothes torn and bloodied, but their spirits unyielding. The battle had tested them in ways they could not have imagined, yet they emerged stronger, a formidable force ready to face whatever challenges lay ahead. The echo of the chain demon's defeat lingered in the air, a reminder of the dangers they would encounter on their quest for the Codex of Whispers. With renewed determination, Rashe, Adran, and Morros pressed onward, their bonds forged in the crucible of battle, bound by a shared purpose to protect their world from the encroaching darkness.

Descending into the depths of the mansion, they encountered powerful guardians protecting the Codex. A gripping battle unfolded as Rashe's enchanting music intertwined with Adran's martial prowess and Morros' deadly precision, culminating in a triumphant victory over the foes.

Finally, the adventurers reached the chamber where the Codex of Whispers rested upon an ancient lectern. However, the tome was guarded by a formidable living rug guardian, animated by arcane forces, ready to defend the sacred knowledge it held. With determination and their combined skills, the party engaged in an intense battle, narrowly overcoming the guardian and securing the Codex.

As the party approached the chamber housing the Codex of Whispers, an eerie aura surrounded the ancient lectern. Unbeknownst to them, a living rug guardian stood in the center of the room – an enigmatic and fearsome creature brought to life by powerful arcane forces. The room's dim light flickered, casting eerie shadows that danced along the walls, creating an air of suspense for the impending clash.

Rashe, Adran, and Morros readied themselves, knowing that something formidable awaited them in this chamber. In a synchronized motion, they prepared their weapons and positions, with the bard raising their lute while the monk and assassin poised for swift action.

Suddenly, without warning, the guardian sprang into action, its woven tendrils lashing out like ferocious snakes. The rug's patterns seemed to shift with a life of their own, weaving and striking with uncanny precision. Adran's keen reflexes allowed them to dodge the initial onslaught gracefully, evading the attacks like a leaf carried by the wind. Meanwhile, Morros vanished into the shadows, relying on their rogue instincts to find the right moment to strike.

Rashe's fingers danced skillfully across the strings of the lute, weaving enchanting melodies that resonated throughout the chamber. Little did they know that their music disrupted the rug guardian's movements, momentarily slowing its assault. Seizing the opportunity, Adran launched a flurry of swift strikes, their fists moving like an unstoppable tempest, connecting with the guardian's ethereal form.

As the battle raged on, two powerful cult guards emerged from the shadows, adorned in dark robes and armed with gleaming blades. With sinister grins, the guards attacked with deadly precision, their weapons aimed to strike the adventurers down.

Morros skillfully slipped past the guards' defenses, delivering swift and lethal strikes, each blow finding its mark with precision. Meanwhile, Rashe's enchanting melodies grew more fervent, empowering their allies with renewed strength and resolve. Adran channeled their inner ki, moving with astonishing speed and grace, countering the guards' strikes with martial finesse.

The room echoed with the clash of steel, the harmony of Rashe's music, and the eerie wails of the guardian. The battle was intense, with the outcome hanging in the balance, but the adventurers fought with an unwavering determination fueled by their unity and shared purpose.

As the dust settled, the rug guardian's ethereal form flickered like a dying flame and finally succumbed to the relentless assault. With one final strike from Morros' blade, the guardian was vanquished, leaving only the faint echoes of its former presence in the air.

The two cult guards, though formidable adversaries, were no match for the combined might of Rashe, Adran, and Morros. With a well-timed attack, the rogue assassin expertly incapacitated one of the guards while the bard's empowering music bolstered the monk's resolve. Adran's fists became a blur of motion, delivering a series of powerful blows that rendered the second guard helpless.

As the dust settled, the adventurers stood victorious, their clothes tattered, and their bodies weary, but their spirits triumphant. The Codex of Whispers lay before them, finally within their grasp, its secrets waiting to be unveiled. United by their indomitable spirit and unyielding bond, Rashe the bard, Adran the monk, and Morros the rogue assassin had overcome insurmountable odds, but their journey was far from over. With the Codex in their possession, a new chapter of adventure and danger awaited them, and the fate of the realm hung in the balance. Now burdened with their hard-won prize, the party had to make their daring escape.

A glimmer of hope arose as they stumbled upon a concealed passage beneath the mansion's foundation. The hidden tunnel beckoned like a secret ally, promising escape from the clutches of their foes. Each twist and turn led them deeper into the darkness, the damp walls of the labyrinthine sewers of Kelrabith echoing with the sounds of rushing water and their own breaths.

As they traversed the gloomy tunnels, they knew that their adventure was far from over. The Codex they now carried held unparalleled power, capable of reshaping the world if wielded by the wrong hands. The Baatorian cult's nefarious reach extended beyond the confines of the mansion, and they were now in possession of a key that could either spell salvation or doom.

However, Rashe, Adran, and Morros refused to falter in the face of uncertainty. The weight of responsibility rested heavy upon their shoulders, but they understood that this was just the beginning of their journey. The Codex needed to be delivered into the capable hands of Averill Kelrabith, a figure of great importance in the realm. With each step, they braced themselves for the challenges ahead, knowing that their actions would shape the course of their own future and the fate of the world.

They couldn't afford to dwell on the unknown, not when their mission demanded resolve and unity. Clutching the Codex tightly, their hearts beating as one, they pressed on, guided by their unwavering determination and trust in each other. As they emerged from the sewers of Kelrabith, their adventure entered a new phase, fraught with peril and unforeseen consequences. But the party remained undeterred, their resolve firm, ready to face whatever awaited them on the path ahead. As the party made their way through the city to meet with Averill at the base of the Moonlight Sanctuary they could hear the alarm being raised from the mansion and the search for them had begun.The weight of the Codex of Whispers in their hands was a testament to the daunting task before them, yet it was also a testament to the strength of their bond and the valor that would carry them through the trials that lay ahead.

Chapter 5

T he city streets were a flurry of activity as Rashe, Adran, and Morros hurried towards the rendezvous point at the base of the Moonlight Sanctuary. With each step they took, the distant echoes of the mansion's alarms reverberated through the city, a haunting reminder that their daring escape had not gone unnoticed. Panic and urgency hung heavy in the air, and the party knew that they were now fugitives, hunted by the relentless Baatorian cult.

Crowds of curious onlookers gathered, whispering amongst themselves as the news of the mansion's turmoil spread like wildfire. Guards and cult followers canvassed the streets, their eyes scanning for any sign of the elusive adventurers. Each alley and shadowy corner became a potential trap, and the party had to tread with caution to avoid detection.

Adran's keen senses helped them navigate through the crowd, adeptly blending in like a shadow amidst the chaos. Morros' agility ensured they moved swiftly and silently, their movements like a phantom's in the night. Rashe, though anxious, remained composed, using their charm to divert attention away from their group while keeping a watchful eye on their surroundings.

As they approached the Moonlight Sanctuary, the party felt a sense of both relief and trepidation. The imposing structure of the sanctuary loomed above them, an ancient haven of knowledge and protection. The Moonlight Sanctuary had stood as a beacon of hope against darkness, but now, it became their refuge, a sanctuary in name and purpose.

As they reached the base of the sanctuary, Averill Kelrabith, a wise and powerful figure, awaited them with a calm demeanor that belied the urgency of the situation. The meeting was brief, and the Codex of Whispers was entrusted into the hands of Averill, who understood the gravity of its power and the responsibility that came with safeguarding it. He handed the party their purse of gold before he quickly made his exit.

Their mission complete, the party turned their attention to the uncertain future that lay before them. The city around them teemed with life, but they knew that they had become fugitives, hunted by the Baatorian cult and surrounded by uncertainty. Yet, the trust and camaraderie they had forged on their journey bolstered their spirits.

As they disappeared into the sanctuary, they knew that their actions had set in motion a series of events that would shape the realm's destiny. The alarms that echoed through the city marked the beginning of a new chapter, one filled with danger, adventure, and a fight for the survival of light against darkness. Rashe, Adran, and Morros steeled themselves, knowing that their journey was far from over, and they would face whatever challenges lay ahead with the unity and courage that had brought them this far.

While searching for an exit they encountered a group of monks and clerics of Ogmios; this not so chance meeting filled Rashe, Adran, and Morros with a mix of relief and concern. While they were relieved that the Codex of Whispers was no longer in their possession, the news that it had been given to someone even more malevolent than the Baatorian cult leader sent shivers down their spines.

The monks and clerics were deeply distressed by the revelation, knowing the dire consequences that the dark wielder of the Codex could bring upon the realm.

Without hesitation, the monks and clerics made it their solemn duty to protect the adventurers who had unknowingly stumbled upon this dangerous affair. Aware that the cult and their malevolent associate would soon be on their trail, the holy protectors vowed to escort Rashe, Adran, and Morros out of Kelrabith and away from the reach of the sinister forces. They hurriedly guided the party through a concealed underground passage that led them to a hidden exit in a field where Kazalath (Kaz) Daywanderer Elanakume, the Goliath barbarian, awaited them with powerful steeds. The Goliath's presence was awe-inspiring, a tower of strength and resolve. Kazalath had earned a reputation as a skilled tracker and protector, known for his unwavering loyalty to the cause of good.

With a somber expression, the monks and clerics spoke of Kazalath's mission to lead them far north, across the treacherous sea, where they would find sanctuary in lands untouched by the Baatorian cult's darkness. Time was of the essence, and the adventurers placed their trust in Kazalath's capable hands. Mounting the steeds, they galloped across the field, their hearts heavy with the knowledge of what they had left behind in Kelrabith. As they journeyed northward, the city's imposing silhouette faded into the distance, the looming threat of the Codex of Whispers and the malevolent wielder casting a lingering shadow.

Over mountains and through valleys, they rode, each passing day taking them farther from the walls of Kelrabith. They drew closer to the coast of the Aureglacier Ocean and their next destination. The Aureglacier Ocean was a realm of wonder and mystery in itself, where sailors and adventurers embark on daring voyages to explore its diverse shores and uncover the secrets hidden beneath its depths. The convergence of warm and cold waters creates a mesmerizing display of ever-changing landscapes, from palm-fringed tropical islands in the south to frosty fjords and glaciers in the north.

They arrived in the bustling coastal city of Seafall Harbor on the western coast of the Aureglacier Ocean. This vibrant and enchanting city boasts a lively ships port, where vessels from distant lands dock to trade goods, share stories, and embark on daring adventures across the vast seas. The city's maritime legacy and proximity to the ocean make it a hub of commerce, culture, and opportunity, attracting travelers, traders, and adventurers alike to its shores.

As the adventurers arrived in Seafall Harbor, Kazalath emphasized the importance of subtlety and blending in. With the cult's members potentially lurking in the city, they needed to avoid drawing attention to themselves. Kazalath assured them that he would secure their passage on a ship bound for the city of Frostwood Haven, where the ice meets the grass in the far north.

Following Kazalath's instructions, Rashe, Adran, and Morros dispersed into the bustling city, adopting personas that would allow them to seamlessly blend into the diverse crowd. Each step was deliberate, every interaction carefully chosen, as they kept a watchful eye on their surroundings.

As night began to descend upon Seafall Harbor, the adventurers reconvened at the Coastal Breeze Tavern, where Kazalath would reveal their plans for passage. The tavern's cozy atmosphere and friendly faces offered a brief respite from the tension that hung in the air.

Kazalath arrived shortly after, his commanding

presence drawing nods of recognition from the party. He shared that he had secured their passage on a reputable ship, its captain known for his trustworthiness and familiarity with the treacherous northern waters. Gathering around a dimly lit table in the corner, they poured over maps and discussed the route to Frostwood Haven. They knew it would be a treacherous journey, but the reward of evading the cult's clutches and potentially uncovering the truth behind the Codex of Whispers spurred them onward.

As nightfall deepened, Kazalath revealed his alternative means of travel. Understanding the need to remain inconspicuous, he opted for a different route and would meet them outside of Frostwood Haven upon their arrival. With plans in place, the adventurers bid farewell to the Coastal Breeze Tavern, venturing into the cool night air with renewed determination. The path ahead was uncertain, fraught with danger, but they were united in purpose and resolve.

In the city where the ice meets the grass, Frostwood Haven, their destinies would converge once more. The unknown awaited them, but they had one another and the assurance of Kazalath's guidance to light their way through the darkness. As they stepped into the night, their hearts were filled with anticipation, knowing that their journey to Frostwood Haven would mark the beginning of an extraordinary chapter in their quest to protect the realm from the clutches of darkness and unearth the secrets of the Codex of Whispers.

Chapter 6

O nce safely aboard the Stormrider, a majestic and grand sailing ship that cuts through the waves with ease, they checked in with Captain Stormwind and were made to feel at ease for they would be making for sea soon and lengthening the distance from the Baatorian cult. The Stormrider was a symbol of freedom and exploration, a beacon of hope for those who seek to chart new courses and discover the wonders that lie beyond the horizon. Captain Seraphina Stormwind was known far and wide for her remarkable skills as a captain, her uncanny ability to navigate through even the most perilous waters, and her fearless leadership in the face of adversity. Her crew trusts her implicitly, as she has proven time and again her dedication to their safety and the success of their voyages. With a reputation for charting unexplored territories and discovering hidden treasures, Captain Seraphina Stormwind commands both respect and admiration among sailors and adventurers alike.

As the party settled into their accommodations aboard the Stormrider, they found themselves pleasantly surprised by the ship's grandeur and comfort. Captain Seraphina Stormwind had ensured that their stateroom was spacious and well-appointed, providing them with a haven of respite amidst their daring voyage. The party marveled at the craftsmanship and attention to detail that went into the ship's design, a testament to the Captain's commitment to her crew's well-being.

During the initial days of sailing, the seas remained calm and inviting, allowing the adventurers to acclimate to life at sea. They relished in exploring the vast vessel, mingling with the crew, and savoring the sense of camaraderie that permeated the ship. The Stormrider was more than just a mode of transportation; it was a community bound by the shared purpose of exploration and adventure.

Amidst their exploration, Adran's keen senses caught sight of another wood elf monk, accompanied by a group of armed sailors who appeared to be protectively escorting him. Adran's curiosity was piqued, and he was eager to make the acquaintance of another of his kind. Despite the initial resistance from the guard, Adran's genuine curiosity and respectful demeanor eventually broke down the barriers. Bevin, sensing Adran's sincerity, intervened and insisted on allowing Adran to approach. As Adran and Bevin exchanged friendly greetings, a connection sparked between them, and they quickly found common ground in their shared heritage as wood elf monks.

Bevin recognized Adran's genuine intentions and saw in him a fellow seeker of knowledge and wisdom. He appreciated Adran's eagerness to learn and his openness to new friendships. As they conversed, Bevin sensed a kindred spirit in Adran and felt a sense of camaraderie that extended beyond words.

As Adran's friendship with Bevin flourished, it quickly became evident that the bond they formed had a profound impact on the entire party. The camaraderie between the four adventurers, Adran, Bevin, Morros, and Rashe, grew stronger with each passing day. Their shared experiences and the trials they faced together on the Stormrider forged a connection that was unbreakable.

Adran's unwavering determination, Bevin's calming presence, Morros' keen wit, and Rashe's en-

chanting melodies complemented each other per-
fectly, making them a formidable team. They
became known among the ship's crew as "The
Fortuitous Few," a title that spoke of their extraordinary luck and their ability to overcome challenges
that fate threw their way.

The adventures they shared aboard the Stormrider
further strengthened their friendship. Together,
they navigated through treacherous storms, battled
fierce sea creatures, and discovered hidden islands
teeming with wonders. Every step of the journey,
they supported and relied on one another, and their
shared triumphs and moments of joy strengthened
their bond.

In the evenings, they gathered on the deck, gazing
at the stars and sharing stories of their pasts and
dreams for the future. They found solace in each
other's company, knowing they were not alone in
this vast and mysterious world.

As the Stormrider continued its voyage, The Fortuitous Few became a beacon of hope and inspiration
for the ship's crew. Their unwavering unity and
determination instilled a sense of confidence in the
entire crew, creating a harmonious and supportive
environment on board.

Captain Seraphina Stormwind watched with pride as the adventurers flourished under the banner of The Fortuitous Few. Their friendship had transcended mere companionship; they had become a family, bound by shared experiences and a common purpose.

As they sailed further into the unknown, the Fortuitous Few faced new challenges, but they did so with the knowledge that they had each other's backs. Their camaraderie and unity were their greatest strength, and together, they were ready to face whatever destiny had in store for them.

The Stormrider and The Fortuitous Few continued to chart new courses, embracing the spirit of freedom and exploration that the ship represented. With Captain Seraphina Stormwind at the helm and the unbreakable bond of The Fortuitous Few, the ship sailed boldly into the horizon, ready to uncover the mysteries that awaited them in the vast and wondrous seas of their fantastical D&D world.

Under Captain Seraphina Stormwind's guidance, the Stormrider continued its voyage, cutting through the waves with grace and ease. The ship became a home away from home for the party, a sanctuary as they ventured into the unknown, drawn by the allure of uncharted territories and hidden treasures.

With every passing day, the Stormrider and its diverse crew forged ahead, guided by the winds of destiny and the spirit of exploration. As the adventurers sailed deeper into the vast and mysterious seas, they knew that the journey ahead held both challenges and wonders, and they were determined to face it all with the unwavering spirit of the Stormrider and the fearless leadership of Captain Seraphina Stormwind.

Chapter 7

As the sky darkened and the winds howled, the once tranquil sea transformed into a tempestuous and unpredictable force. The Stormrider began to pitch and roll, challenging the skill of even the most seasoned sailors. Adran, Rashe, Morros, and Bevin stood on deck, their eyes fixed on the turbulent waters before them.

"Looks like we're in for a rough ride," Adran shouted over the roaring winds, squinting through the rain. "We better hold on tight."

"Indeed," Rashe replied, clinging to the railing. "This storm came out of nowhere. Captain Seraphina must be working hard to steer the ship through this."

Morros, tightening his grip on the mast, chimed in, "Let's hope her navigational skills can steer us clear of any danger. We need to be prepared for anything."

Bevin, ever the calm and composed presence,

assessed the situation, "Agreed. The sea can be unpredictable, but we must trust in the Stormrider and the crew. Our unity will see us through."

As the ship continued to battle the raging waves, the party members exchanged determined glances, their bond of friendship stronger than ever. The Stormrider's crew worked tirelessly to keep the ship steady, and the adventurers knew they had to stay alert and ready to assist if needed. Together, they braced themselves for the challenges ahead, knowing that their unwavering teamwork would carry them through this formidable storm.The wind howled and the rain lashed against their faces, but Adran, Rashe, Morros, and Bevin stood resolute, united in their determination to face whatever challenges the storm threw their way. Each member of The Fortuitous Few relied on the other, knowing that together they were a force to be reckoned with.

As the waves crashed over the ship and the storm raged on, the party held their ground, weathering the tempest with unwavering resolve. They knew that storms were an inevitable part of their adventurous journey, and in times of turmoil, their friendship would be their greatest anchor.

Through the crashing waves and howling winds, The Fortuitous Few stood strong, bound by the spirit of camaraderie that had brought them together in the first place. They knew that no matter what challenges lay ahead, they would face them with courage, unity, and the unwavering support of their newfound friends.

And so, as the storm raged on, Adran, Rashe, Morros, and Bevin stood together, ready to brave the elements and sail onward, for the sea of adventure held both danger and wonders, and they were determined to embrace it all as one united front.

With the same speed that the storm had descended upon them, it now dispersed, leaving behind calmer waters and clearer skies. From the crow's nest, the lookout's voice rang out, "SOMETHING IN THE WATER STARBOARD SIDE!"

The chaos and danger of the Sea of Souls unfolded rapidly as the sea hags emerged from the depths, their malevolent intent clear. The crew on the ship sprang into action, but it was too late for Adran, who was yanked overboard and met with a brutal impact against the ship's rail and the unforgiving sea below. The sea hags were infamous for their merciless attacks, leaving no trace of their victims behind.

"Rashe, Adran was pulled overboard!" Morros yelled, his voice filled with panic and desperation, urgently alerting Rashe to Adran's perilous fate.

Without hesitation, Rashe, a drakonisk bard with a deep bond with his best friend, leaped overboard in pursuit. Bevin, the agile and skilled forest elf monk and cleric, swiftly followed, their movements synchronized as they dove gracefully into the water, leaving barely a ripple in their wake.

As they submerged into the frigid, murky waters, Rashe and Bevin scanned their surroundings, their eyes darting to and fro in a desperate search for their friend. Adran's life hung in the balance, and they were determined to rescue him from the clutches of the malevolent sea hags. Spotting the sea hag that had seized Adran, Bevin summoned his inner Ki and propelled himself forward through the turbulent water, striking the hag with his staff, forcing her to relinquish her grip on Adran and pushing her away. Rashe wasted no time, grabbing hold of his friend and using all his strength to propel them both back to the surface.

As they emerged above water, Rashe frantically checked Adran's condition, relieved to find him alive but in critical condition. Meanwhile, Morros, fiercely determined to protect his friends, wielded the ship's ballista and fired with deadly precision, piercing another sea hag's cold heart.

Bevin surfaced, keeping a vigilant eye on Adran, using his cantrip of life to stabilize him and ensure he clung to life until he could be healed properly. Amid the chaos of battle, Bevin's unwavering focus on his friend's well-being shielded him from the sea hag's death stare, allowing him to stay unharmed.

The struggle continued as the sea hags persisted in their bloodthirsty assault, but the bond between the trio proved formidable. Together, they fought for their lives and for each other, their hearts beating as one. The Sea of Souls had shown its treacherous nature, but the strength of their camaraderie and unwavering determination would serve as a beacon of hope amid the darkest depths.

The battle with the sea hags had taken its toll on Rashe and his companions, but their camaraderie and resourcefulness had prevailed. Despite the minimal damage inflicted upon him, Rashe's swift underwater maneuver had proved decisive. With a powerful thunderclap spell, he caused havoc among the sea hags, amplifying the damage in the water. The ship's ballista struck true, delivering a deadly blow that severed one hag's head from her body, while Bevin's scimitar left another hag disarmed and defeated.

As the third hag vanished into the depths of the Sea of Souls, the immediate focus turned to Adran's well-being. With the assistance of the ship's crew, Rashe managed to hoist his injured friend back onto the ship. Bevin, ever the healer, diligently focused his energy on mending Adran's wounds. The party knew that time and rest were essential for Adran's recovery, and they ensured he was comfortable below decks, watched over by Morros.

With the immediate danger past, Bevin retreated below decks to regain his strength, knowing that he would need to tend to Adran once more. The hours passed, and Bevin returned, his divine healing touch reviving Adran's spirit and mending his battered body.

As the ship sailed northward along the Sevain Coast, the days passed uneventfully. The danger of the sea hag encounter still lingered in their thoughts, but the knowledge of their resilience and unity gave them strength. Rashe's soothing melodies lifted their spirits during the journey, and Adran grew stronger with each passing day, thanks to Bevin's unwavering care and healing abilities.

As they approached the northern part of the Sevain Coast, anticipation filled the air. Frostwood Haven was within reach, and their quest to uncover the mysteries of the Codex of Whispers would continue. The adventures they had already shared bound them together, forging an unbreakable bond as they faced the unknown that awaited them in the icy lands ahead. The Aureglacier Ocean had proven to be a realm of both beauty and peril, but with their hearts united and their spirits resilient, they were prepared for whatever challenges lay ahead on their epic journey.

Chapter 8

The ship dropped anchor off the coast just south of Frostwood Haven at sunset. The adventurers disembarked from the ship that brought them north on what they hope was the last part of their journey. This was farther north than most of the members of this party have ever been. However, none of them know what lies ahead, and they hope that their newfound friend, Kaz, will be able to assist them in settling into a new life. Hard to believe that just a week ago this party that was three had now turned into a party of five after just a simple adventure to recover a book.

Adran, Morros, Rashe, and Bevin slowly walk to a camp that Kaz has set up for their arrival. A fire burned with a pot of sweet-smelling stew, and tents for each of them, including the guards and cook, had already been set up. "You would think you just fought off a horde of orcs the way you four are walking," Kaz said as he laughed.

Morros replies, "more like a group of sea hags."

"Looks like I missed all the fun," Kaz replied.

"Well, dry ground and good food are what you have now," Markov, the orc cook says as he poured goblets of wine and scooped bowls of stew for everyone.

When it comes to a group of adventures, there was usually a common factor that brings them together, a past wrong to be righted, or a common enemy that needs to be outed. With this group, the commonality seemed to be mostly the need for adventure and a group to belong to. Everyone in this unlikely band brought a certain something to the group, and everyone still hid what was most dear to them until it was needed. Not everything about a person needs to be shared, even with those they trust the most. Having a secret skill, feat, background, or even a name everyone does not know was how all people maintain their individuality.

At the campsite, everyone gathered with their goblets, bowls, and seats. They shared a meal, indulged in conversation, and eventually settled into a state of relaxation. Among them was Bevin, a recent addition to the party. Grateful for the company, he expressed his thanks to Marvok before quietly enjoying his food, all the while observing his new companions. As he looked around, a question echoed in his mind, "Are these the ones I am meant to protect, to form a family with, to refine my skills alongside?"

Taking a sip from his goblet, the warmth of the red wine triggered a memory from his monk training days. It reminded him of his old friend and training partner, Reston, who had an affinity for red wine. Bevin recalled the first time he had tried it - after an exhausting staff training session when Reston had conveniently forgotten to bring water, leaving only red wine as their beverage option. With the closest water source being miles away, Bevin had given in and partaken in the wine. Surprisingly, he found it soothing and comforting, the warmth spreading through him from the inside out.

Reston had claimed that the wine made meditation easier, but Bevin couldn't help but feel that his friend needed it to find stillness since he was always restless. Unlike the other Wood Elves in his training, Bevin possessed a natural calmness and tranquility that set him apart. The Masters of Silvanus temple recognized this gift, attributing it to the blessings of the Oak Father, meant for those chosen to aid and educate others.

While the wine seemed to have a calming effect on most people, for Bevin, it merely served as a refreshing indulgence, as he was already naturally composed and serene. He didn't rely on it to find his inner peace, unlike Reston or some others. As the memory faded, Bevin returned to the present, feeling content in the company of his new companions, eager to discover how his unique abilities and calm demeanor could contribute to their adventures together.

"Did you doze off, elf?" Rashe's voice boomed with amusement, breaking the silence around the campfire.

Bevan smiled and replied, "No, my friend. The wine just stirred a memory I wanted to revisit for a moment."

A young guard couldn't resist making a playful remark, "Ah, red wine always makes me think of the enchanting ladies in Frostwood Haven."

Teasing laughter erupted as another guard chimed in, "Yeah, but you only dare to look, not touch!"

As the banter carried on, the guards immersed themselves in the merriment, leaving the young guard feeling a bit perplexed and lost for words. He mustered a confused retort, "Um, well, I mean… I just meant… you know what I mean!"

His attempt at defending himself lacked the same wit and charm as the others', and he couldn't quite find the right words to match their playful banter. His cheeks flushed with a mix of embarrassment and amusement as the laughter around the campfire continued. Despite feeling a bit out of place, he couldn't help but enjoy the lighthearted atmosphere, realizing that he was slowly becoming a part of this spirited group of companions.

Marvok, the seasoned member of the group, offered some sagely advice, "It's alright, young one. Even we were once clueless about those ladies. But stay clear of their pursuit, and you won't need to empty your pockets on the healer every week!"

Kaz, the imposing and handsome figure among them, joined in with a chuckle, "Yes, even the mighty and attractive Kaz was once young and naive. Now, I've learned my lesson - never get involved with any woman these guys have been with!"

The campfire crackled, and laughter echoed into the night, forming a bond among the companions. In this light-hearted moment, they found solace from the challenges of their journey, sharing stories, and weaving memories together as they continued to forge their path through the world.

As Kaz made his humorous comment, his deep, booming laughter filled the air, resonating like thunder in the camp. Standing at an imposing height of 7 feet and 5 inches, he was a gargantuan figure, a barbarian hailing from a tribe nestled in the Spine of The World. His pale bluish skin and bald head were a testament to the harsh environment he grew up in. Kaz's usual attire consisted of minimal animal skins, even in the freezing cold of Ten Towns.

After his jest, he excused himself with a hearty laugh and made his way towards the edge of the tree line for some privacy. As he relieved himself, his mind wandered back to memories of home and his time as a soldier in his tribe. He reminisced about running alongside his fellow warriors, defending and hunting for the entire tribe. But amidst those recollections, there was a bittersweet memory that lingered.

There was a girl in the tribe, someone to whom Kaz's future was once bonded. They had dreams and expectations for their life together. However, fate took an unexpected turn during a raid that Kaz led. The outcome was not what he and his family had hoped for, and it left him with a sense of responsibility for the events that transpired.

Now, he traveled the lands as a wanderer, lending his aid to those in need who couldn't defend themselves. Despite being welcomed back to his tribe on visits, he knew he could never fully be a part of it again. The weight of his past actions and the choices he made had forever changed the course of his life.

As he returned to the campfire, the laughter and camaraderie of his companions greeted him warmly. Kaz might have a past shrouded in shadows, but in the company of these fellow adventurers, he found a sense of purpose and a chance to make amends for the mistakes of his past. The memories of his tribe and the girl he once loved remained a part of him, shaping the man he had become - a compassionate protector, dedicated to helping others find hope and safety in a world full of challenges.

The night continued with good wine, a warm fire, and the further building of friendship. No one asked the questions Kaz expected to answer, but then again, it seemed they all just wanted to unwind and relax. The guard set the watch, the cook finished cleaning up, and left what stew was not eaten in a covered cast iron pot for anyone to serve themselves.

As the aroma of the fire and stew wafted through the air, memories of home and bygone days flooded Rashe's mind. Sitting there, he found solace in recollections of his youth, spent with his beloved family. Unconsciously, his fingers began to dance upon the ocarina, playing a tender melody he had learned during his days at the bardic school. This tune harked back to a time when he was known as Vrjefka, the name bestowed upon him by his parents. It was a name reserved for those closest to him, reflecting a side of himself that remained unguarded, with nothing to conceal.

Nowadays, Rashe performed under a different name, as was customary among many bards. Yet, his thoughts wandered to the private corners of his heart, where he kept his deepest secrets hidden from others. Amidst these reflections, a gentle smile graced his drakonisk countenance, contentedly reminiscing about his past.

With gratitude, Markov expressed, "Thank you for the beautiful tune. See you all in the morning." With those words, he bid his companions farewell and retired to his tent, seeking a night's rest. Following suit, the rest of the group made their way to their designated tents, settling in for a peaceful night's sleep.

This night Adran, a wood elf monk, was more restless than usual; dreams of his past filled his head. Adran's memories of his youth are gone, buried long ago for reasons he does not know. He knew that Rashe found him on a shoreline and helped him get healed up. From that day on, he has been a bodyguard and traveling companion to Rashe. Adran had dreams at night that were flashes of his past, but he did not know what they meant, nor did they stay with him long enough to make any sense. He knows that the dragon turtle was vital to him and his past, so he clings to it and learns all he can about the dragon turtle. A smile came to his face as he saw his mother's face, drifting back into a deep meditation. Too bad he will not remember that face when he awakens.

Morros was one of the most mysterious of this band of brothers. He was a Tiefling rogue that does what makes sense to him and benefits him. He sleeps well at night, knowing that his day has been to his advantage and that he has fulfilled the actions that benefited him the most. This was not to say that what he did was averse to his companions or that he did not do all he could to assist his companions, nor was he selfish. Helping those he travels with does benefit him in a way that if they live and prosper, so does he. Somehow helping these companions feels better to him than any others he had traveled with. Morros has yet to figure out what it was about this group he joined that pleases him, but he will stay with them for a while, maybe longer.

Unbeknownst to the other four members of the group, Kaz will leave them for some time as he sets up what could be the adventure of their lifetime and could make or break their time in the Northlands. Adran, Rashe, Morros, and Bevin will have to make their names in this new part of the Sword Coast to make a living for themselves. Kaz will be a beacon in their lives for as long as he can, but he also has a mission of his own that he was driven to complete.

The morning will bring an entirely new start for each of them.

Chapter 9

As the morning light bathed the camp, the delightful scent of bacon, eggs, and coffee filled the air, accompanied by the soldiers' groans as they rose from their tents. The rough night's sleep on the hard ground left them feeling older than their years. Kaz sat calmly on a log, enjoying his breakfast and the tranquility of the early hours. Alongside him, Markov marveled at the peaceful clouds, likening them to a city untouched by human presence.

As the party members emerged from their tents, Markov thoughtfully served up breakfast and the tantalizing coffee with its mysterious aroma, unparalleled in all of Liniște.

Kaz addressed the group, informing them that they needed to remain low-key in the area for the next ten days while he attended to important matters. He warned against venturing into Frostwood Haven to avoid any trouble. With a gruff tone, he reminded Rashe to keep a low profile, avoiding any unnecessary attention they had attracted in the past.

Morros reassured Kaz, promising to keep an eye on everyone, but the concern on Kaz's face showed his lingering doubts. Kaz bid them farewell, heading north to complete his mission.

With Kaz gone, Bevin suggested exploring the town to familiarize themselves with the area and locate useful shops. The group agreed, preparing for the outing. The leader of the guard, a formidable figure, assured them that their belongings would be safe under his watch, though this brought both comfort and caution to the group.

As the group of friends strolled towards Frostwood Haven, they immersed themselves in the lively crowd of merchants setting up their carts and makeshift stores along the main street and town square. The marketplace displayed an array of goods, from fresh produce and meats to flowers, trinkets, jewelry, books, potions, and more. Amidst this vibrant scene, Morros couldn't help but be drawn to a tiefling woman selling delicate fabrics, a rare sight as tieflings were not usually merchants. She was tall, slender, and attractive, and their eyes met as she turned her head with a smile. The group continued on their way, but Morros felt her gaze on him as they rounded a corner, pondering the possibility of returning to her shop later.

As they rounded the corner, a troubling scene unfolded before them. The city guard had pinned a young human man against the wall and proceeded to search him roughly, seemingly intent on finding any reason to arrest him. An elderly lady, standing by her small shop, accused the young man of stealing a silver box.

The lieutenant of the guard commanded, "Search every inch of him and make sure he wasn't hiding anything."

Despite the accusations, the guard searching the man found nothing. He hesitated, suggesting, "Should we take him to jail and search him more thoroughly?"

Adran, always observant, couldn't ignore the situation. He asked the shop owner, "Was the box in your hand the one you're looking for, ma'am?"

Startled, the shop owner hastily concealed the box in her pocket and snapped, "Mind your own business!"

Unfazed, Adran faced the lieutenant and the shop owner, inquiring, "What are you putting in your pocket?"

Nervously, the shop owner admitted, "Well, I guess it was my mistake. I am getting old and must not have realized I had the box the whole time."

The lieutenant sighed in exasperation, scolding her, "Release him, and next time you make a mistake like that, you will be taxed for wasting the guard's time." He nodded at Adran in acknowledgment.

The young man, now free, expressed his gratitude to Adran, saying, "Thank you, sir," before heading towards the market square.

Rashe quietly reminded the group, "Keep a low profile," as they continued down the street. Bevin smiled and patted Adran on the shoulder, knowing it held deeper meaning than just a friendly gesture. In the short time they had known each other, Adran had learned that Bevin valued kindness and helping others above all else. This show of support from a fellow monk and wood elf made him feel a sense of belonging, akin to having a proud family member smile upon him.

They continued down the street, making a mental map of where the stores were and which ones they may want to visit later. They feel it was better to know the city's layout before getting into a situation where they need to know how to get out of town in more than one direction. They all know that exits are the difference between life and death when the need arises. This street ends into another street running north and south, but directly across from them was a large and already busy tavern. Even for a bard, it was early to be in a tavern, so they continue to the south, mentally noting that this was where they will be for lunch.

Heading south, the group ventured in the opposite direction they had entered the town. As they progressed, the buildings began to show signs of neglect, and the people appeared more downtrodden. All four of them heightened their alertness, carefully observing every movement on the street. The thoroughfares were filled with people begging for money, and children played amidst the squalor and grime that covered this neglected part of town. It seemed as though those in power had forgotten about this section entirely.

A sense of danger permeated the air, and they felt as though this was the part of town where people could easily vanish, especially if they made a wrong decision about whom to trust. Deciding it was best to turn back and head to the other side of town, they began to retrace their steps. However, their return was met with an unwelcome surprise – a group of male human thugs stepping out in front of them.

One of the thugs sneered, "If you're leaving, you can pay the exit tax you owe since you spent no money in our fair part of town."

Bevin replied, "So, if we buy something in your part of town, we can leave without paying the tax?"

The leader of the thugs laughed and replied, "No,

you will still have to pay to leave."

As the tension rose, Morros raised his hood and deftly vanished into the shadows, unnoticed by anyone. Adran and Bevin tightened their grips on their staffs, positioning themselves in a ready stance. Rashe urged Bevin to reason with the thugs, granting him bardic inspiration. The thugs' faces lit up with malicious glee as they fantasized about overpowering the adventurers and looting them.

Suddenly, Morros emerged from the darkness and launched a surprise attack on the thug at the back. Swift as the wind, he plunged one dagger into the thug's back and slit his throat with the other. Blood gushed from the thug's neck, but he couldn't even cry out, as Morros's precise strikes had pierced his lung and severed his vocal cords. Meanwhile, the lead thug swung his sword, cutting Bevin deeply across the arm, causing blood to spew from the wound.

With a loud "KIHAP," Adran jumped in the air, spun, kicked one of the thugs in the face, and knocked him down. As he hit the ground, Adran landed with another loud "KIHAP" and smashed his opponent's nose with his fist; as the bone crushed, the cartilage ripped from the bone, and blood poured from his nose. The thug lay on the ground choking on his blood and trying to focus through the tears as they streamed out of his eyes and down his face. The thug sluggishly tried to stand, stumbling as he regained his footing and barely got upright and stepped back into a defensive stance with his sword in hand.

Bevin quietly slid forward like he was on ice and plunged his staff forward with a two-handed grip at the thug that cut him. He struck him in the center of his chest and knocked him back and off his feet. As the thug slammed into the ground, Bevin yelled, "KIHAP," catapulting himself in the air with his staff and landing hard on the thug's chest. The leader gasped for a breath as the air was forced out of his lungs and his ribs snapped. Bevin slid back into a defensive stance and readied himself for the next round.

As the fight progressed, Rashe played his ocarina, and the fourth thug of the group was enthralled with his music. The song made the young thug feel like Rashe was the only person who mattered, and he would do anything he asked. As the song continued to caress his eardrums, he ran down the street, jumped off the pier, and swam to the middle of the harbor. The tune overwhelmed him so much that he swam for the open ocean until he heard the music no more. He came to his senses in the middle of the shipping channel. As the young thug looked up, a large galleon slammed into him, knocked him unconscious, and sank to the harbor's bottom. Rashe smiled and turned back towards his friends, ready for the next round.

The thug with the broken nose wiped his eyes and plunged his sword tip first at Adran, piercing him in the shoulder. The blood ran down Adran's arm and pain burned throughout his shoulder, unlike anything he had felt before. As the thug jumped back, Adran spun his staff over his head and landed a solid hit against the thug's head. As the thug stumbled, Adran jumped into the air and landed a solid kick against his back as fire flew out of his foot and engulfed his opponent. The thug fell to the ground writhing in pain and yelling as he burned to death.

The last thug of the group was the leader, and he lay on the ground gasping for breath. Morros slinked forward and put a blade to his neck with a big smile. Bevin, Rashe, and Adran all turned and looked at the beaten leader on the ground near death. Rashe stepped forward and questioned the leader, "so what was that tax we needed to pay?" The leader looked up at him and took one final breath, and blood bubbled out of his mouth as he drowned. Bevin looked around to ensure no others were making their way toward them. All he saw were the beggars and poor huddling against the walls in fear.

Bevin said, "Let the people they have exploited take the loot. We can head back north in town and heal ourselves as we leave these people."

With that, the group turned north and made their way back to the other end of town, noting that this was not a place to return to. Bevin slid a few gold coins out of his pouch and dropped them on the ground in front of a woman and her two young children. He smiled, nodded to her, and said, "May the Oak Father bless you."

Chapter 10

After the party had moved north and lost sight of the other end of town, Adran began to slow and stumble in his steps. He stammered a few more steps, fell to his knees, and said, "Bevin, I think I have been poisoned." He fumbled for his bag and said, "There was a poison antidote potion in a green vile," as he slumped down on his back.

Rashe grabbed the bag and searched for the vile as Bevin laid his hands on Adran and used spare the dying just in case. Rashe produced the vile and uncorked it, and Morros lifted Adran's head, so the green, foul-smelling liquid could be poured into his mouth. Bevin continued to say a prayer and heal his friend as the antidote worked its way down his throat. The healing spell and antidote worked together on Adran as his eyes began to blink, and a smile came over his face. Adran remarked, "I hope this does not become the normal outcome of our encounters."

Rashe chuckled, "getting tired of picking you up

off the ground, old friend."

Morros shook his head and said, "if only you could take the damage as well as you can deal out the attacks."

Bevin laughs, "I guess I need to learn some more healing spells to keep up with your luck."

Rashe laughs, "Maybe we should find a potion shop and stock up on healing and antidote before we go any further."

Adran guffaws along with them all and said, "A good investment for my gold!"

Rashe offers a hand to Adran and lifts him to his feet, and says, "This seems like a good time to get some food and relax a bit in that tavern we saw."

The party exchanged nods of agreement and set off towards the Golden Dragon Tavern. As they meandered through the bustling streets, they encountered various merchants peddling their wares. The diverse town of Frostwood Haven seemed to be a melting pot of races from all over Farnere, some unfamiliar to the party. Amidst the lively scene, a group of children played tag, and one of them accidentally collided with Bevin. Reacting with a playful maneuver, Bevin shielded the child from his pursuers, sending him off in the opposite direction with laughter and glee. The sight brought back fond memories of Bevin's own carefree days playing with friends as a child. Adran noticed the joy on Bevin's face and shared a smile, feeling a sense of familiarity he couldn't quite place.

Upon reaching the tavern, the party scanned the room for an empty table, but the ones offering tactical advantages were already taken. They settled for a spot in the center, passing by tables occupied by dwarves, elves, humans, and a lively gathering of half-orcs. The only other option was a table strewn with dirty dishes and spilled ale, which they wisely avoided. The tavern maiden approached them, inquiring about their order.

Rashe inquired, "What was your finest meal and drink?"

She responded, "Dragon wine was the best drink in the house, along with the Dragon Ale. Our best meal today was the roasted boar, carrots, and potatoes."

Rashe smiled, "The wine and boar sound delightful to me."

The tavern maiden cautioned, "As long as you have ten silver pieces."

Rashe generously handed her two gold pieces, saying, "Keep the glasses of wine coming, and I have more for you."

Adran chimed in, "That sounds perfect. I'll have the same." He also handed her two gold pieces.

Morros grinned and said, "Make it the same for me." He followed suit, handing her two gold pieces.

Bevin, with a simple request, said, "Toast and jam with water, please." He handed her five silver pieces.

To his surprise, the maiden replied, "That will only be two copper pieces for that."

Bevin smiled warmly, saying, "May the Oak Father bless your family."

The maiden looked puzzled but replied, "Okay, I will get your orders for you now."

As the party waited for their meals, they observed the atmosphere in the tavern. Some groups raised their mugs in remembrance of lost companions, while Morros noticed a hooded figure sitting alone in a corner, attracting attention as people approached and exchanged items with them. Morros recognized this figure as the contract intermediary, potentially connected to the rogue's guild in Frostwood Haven. Rashe, on the other hand, took note of the stage at the center, prepared for bards or musicians to entertain the crowd.

Their delicious meals arrived, and they relished the fine wine and clean water, savoring the taste and the respite it brought. Once they had finished, they resolved to find a store renowned for its quality potions. After considering their options, they decided to seek advice from the trustworthy tavern maiden, Ranala, who seemed to have some insight into the local potioneer, Natasha, despite their strained relationship. With their plans set, they awaited Natasha's return, all the while contemplating the opportunities that might arise while staying incognito in Frostwood Haven, eager to make wise choices as they waited for Kaz's return. Since Rashe had caught her smile and asked, "Do you know of a reputable potioneer in town?"

The tavern maiden smiled, "my sister-in-law was probably the best, even though I don't like her one bit."

Rashe chuckled, "well, she must be good if you recommend her but don't like her."

She replied, "She was good to her potions but not so good to me, brother."

Rashe gave an apprehensive look to her, "I am sorry to hear that. Should we not spend our gold at her shop then?"

She replied, "No, she was the best, and at least that will ensure there was money for my brother and nephew if you go there."

Rashe smiled, "Well, where can we find her then? And what was your name?"

She smiled back, "I am Ranala, and you can find her shop east down the main road here and turn north at the second street, Dry Well alley, and look for a sign with Natasha's painted in green on it."

"Thank you, Ranala. Maybe we will see you again." Rashe replied and handed her a silver piece.

The others stood, and each handed Ranala a silver piece for her hospitality and walked out the tavern door. As they headed east down the main road, they noticed more city guards were walking around than usual. They kept to themselves and turned up Dry Well alley toward the potioneer. As they walked up the road a few blocks, they spotted the sign for Natasha's. From the outside, they could see herbs and other plants hanging in the window, either drying out or growing green and fresh. The sign on the door said, "will return soon," so they decided to wait outside the shop for her return. While waiting for the shopkeeper, they discussed what they might do during the next week as they waited for Kaz to return.

Morros had noted that when they were in the tavern, he saw a person that seemed to be a contract intermediary and that maybe they could find some work if anyone was interested. The party mulled it between them and noted that if they could keep a low profile here in Frostwood Haven as Kaz asked them, it would be a good idea to make some money. It was agreed that after they purchased the items they needed, they would return to the tavern and see what the intermediary offered.

Chapter 11

On board the ship, Kala Silverbeard[1], known as "The Scalp Master" from Labrys, found himself in a mysterious situation. He wasn't sure how he ended up on the ship or where it was heading. The steward, Magrius, a kind-hearted human teen, attended to Kala's needs with great care. He found Kala's tales of bounty hunting and his homeland, Labrys, far more interesting than dealing with the usual snobbish rich passengers. Throughout the journey, Magrius ensured Kala had the best cleaning solvents and materials for his mithril plate armor, as well as leather straps to rewrap the handle of his warhammer, "The Skull Crusher." Kala was grateful for the unexpected luxury and security in his cabin, even though he was uncertain about the circumstances that brought

---

[1] Kala Silverbeard and Labrys are a part of "The Gates of Anak'anor" by Topher Metcalf & Walt Allen. They are used with consent from Topher Metcalf.

him here.

One morning, Magrius knocked on Kala's cabin door and greeted him with his usual jovial tone, "Good morning sir! I wanted you to know that we will arrive in Frostwood Haven in three days."

Kala looked intrigued and inquired, "Frostwood Haven? Where was Frostwood Haven located?"

Magrius replied, "Frostwood Haven was north on the Sword Coast, just south of the Spine of the World."

Puzzled, Kala repeated, "North on the Sword Coast, south of the Spine of the World. Would you happen to have a map that you could show me?"

Magrius offered, "I will see if I can get one for you, or maybe we could go to the ship's navigator, and he could show you the map he uses to navigate with." Then he hurried away to find the map.

Kala sat back, deep in thought, and decided against leaving the safety of his cabin until he understood the situation better. He stroked his long, shining beard, trying to make sense of it all.

After a while, Magrius returned with the map and knocked on Kala's door again. "I have a map to show you, sir," he said.

Curious, Kala invited him in, "Come in and show me where we are."

Magrius unrolled the map on the desk in the cabin, explaining about Frostwood Haven being a large town known as "The City of Sails," with over fifteen thousand people living there and access to almost anything one could want. As Magrius continued, Kala used his cartography tools to make a crude copy of the map, hoping to understand his location better. He had more questions than before, but he didn't want to appear lost or vulnerable.

Over the next few days, Kala rested and finished the repairs on his armor and weapons. He knew he was now ready for anything that might come his way, especially if he encountered any elves, as dwarves and elves were mortal enemies where he came from – Labrys. This might pose some challenges on the Sword Coast.

As the ship approached the port of Frostwood Haven, Kala donned his armor, strapped his shield to his back, and grabbed his Warhammer. Before leaving the cabin, he handed Magrius two gold pieces, thanking him for his excellent service. Magrius was visibly surprised by the gesture, as he had never seen so much gold at once. He smiled and thanked Kala in return, appreciating the kind gesture from the mysterious bounty hunter.

Chapter 12

As the Fortuitous Few are still waiting on the potioneer to open, a large galleon named "Tainted Rose" pulled into port carrying passengers from different parts of the world. This ship comes to Frostwood Haven once a year and usually has more interesting passengers than the usual ships that pull in. The galleon was larger than any other ship on the sea, twice the size of a normal galleon, and makes a journey that took one year to circumnavigate the globe of Daruta. Occasionally some passengers come from places unknown to this realm or even this plane of existence.

As the ship docks and the passengers begin to disembark into Frostwood Haven, Kala overhears several of them talking about The Golden Dragon Tavern. Since he was unsure where he was or where he was going, this seemed like a good place to start. He followed the crowd that appeared to know where the tavern was. As he makes his way down the road, he sees the buildings here are well-kept, clean, and very ornately detailed. This seemed to be a city of wealth and power. Down the road, about a mile from the dock, the sign for the Golden Dragon Tavern hangs brightly painted to where it almost looks to be illuminated in the middle of the day. Kala passes through the tavern door, and as he does, he feels his stomach turn a bit and feels unsteady on his feet. It almost felt like someone nudged him from behind, but it only lasted a brief moment.

Kala gathers his wits quickly and looks around the tavern. The inside of the tavern seemed to be larger on the inside than the building was on the outside. To the left of the entrance was a long bar with twenty stools full of humans sitting and drinking various drinks. In the tavern's center was a large round wooden stage with instruments set up as if a band was ready to play. All around the stage were tables filled with patrons. A group of half-orcs had drinks, ate, and told tales of their adventures in their own language. There was also a group of elves quietly eating that caught Kala's attention. Several tables were filled with dwarves drinking, singing, and eating. Off to the back of the tavern was a row of booths filled with humans eating brunch, but the last booth had a hooded figure sitting alone. The hooded figure had a table full of small sacks, and stacks of parchments.

A half-orc approached the hooded figure and quietly spoke to him. The man handed the half-orc a small sack and a parchment. Kala realizes that this was the contract intermediary for the area and decides he needs to prove himself so he can get some work. In Labrys, you must prove yourself to get a contract, and since he did not know where he was nor was he known, he felt he needed to prove himself to the hooded figure giving out the jobs and gold. Kala needed to think fast and show the intermediary what he was capable of, and he needed to do it now.

Kala gripped his warhammer tight and looked at the elves, his mortal enemy, sitting nearby ran and swung at them as they sat and drank. The first unsuspecting elf was struck so hard by The Scalp Master that he and his chair lifted off the ground and slammed hard on the floor. The elf was in a daze as Kala swung his warhammer around and struck him a second time, crushing his skull and killing him instantly. The other two elves looked on with astonishment and were frozen with fear.

Kala looked at the dwarves and yelled, "WHO'S WITH ME!"

The dwarves looked on, holding their drinks and staring in amazement at what they were witnessing, as was everyone else in the tavern. Kala saw that no one was moving to join him in his attack.

Kala said to the elves, "we gonna finish this, or you gonna run?"

One of the elves jumped up, pulled his sword, and replied, "You will pay for the death of my brother!" He swung his sword, hitting Kala on the breastplate but doing nothing to him.

The third elf jumped up with his mace in hand and yelled, "SPIRITS GUIDE ME!" and struck Kala in the arm. The mace lit up bright yellow and knocked Kala to the side and caused him some slight damage.

Kala laughs and replies, "finish it, I guess, was your answer." He swung his Warhammer at the elf with the sword and landed a hit to his chest, knocking the wind out of him. Kala continued his attack by striking the elf in the head, landing a critical blow that killed him on impact.

The last elf said, "What did my brethren do to you?" as he once again swung his mace and struck Kala in the arm with a bright yellow glow of sparks that exploded from the impact. Kala was knocked sideways, but the damage did not stop him.

Kala furrowed his brow deepened his stance lifted his warhammer, and struck the elf in the shoulder, which disarmed him. Now the elf stood weaponless in front of him, his shoulder hanging there, broken and useless. Kala took a breath and, with a loud war cry, spun and struck the elf on the side of his head so hard that it tore the flesh from his neck and almost severed his head. The elf flew back six feet and rolled across the tavern floor. During all the commotion, patrons had begun running for the exit. The hooded figure gathered his things and jumped up from the booth as Kala turned and looked at him.

Kala said, "Did I prove my worth for a job with you?"

Tal, the hooded figure, replied, "I could use someone with your skillset, but first, we must hide you from the city guard. Follow me."

Tal made for the door, and Kala followed close behind. As Tal looked up and down the streets, he heard the city guard yelling for people to move and knew they were close. Tal ran across the road and down the small road across from the tavern, with Kala following close behind. After running about three blocks, they turned into a small alley between two buildings. Tal ducked behind some old crates, looked around, placed his hand on the brick wall, mumbled something, and a secret door opened. Tal pushed Kala through the door and followed him in. The door shut behind them and was not visible due to the number of shelves lining the wall.

Once the door closed behind them, Tal lit an oil lamp that hung on the wall. In the dim light, Kala could see that the room was a storage room filled with books, boxes, bags, and chests. It smelled of aromatic spices and mold all mixed together. There was a table in the middle of the room with two small chairs and a deck of cards. Nothing in this room gave the sense that someone lived there, just that it was used to hide things and people away.

Tal said, "You can hide here until I can get you out of the city. Was there anything that you want while you are here?"

Kala replied, "How about a dwarven female companion."

Tal said, "I will see what I can do. In the meantime, there was food and water in that chest, and if you want to sleep, there was a bed on the other side of the shelves in the north corner. Just give them a push, and it will open."

Kala nodded at Tal as he opened the secret door leading out into the ally. Tal closed the secret door behind him, and it seemed that the door was never there. Kala sat down and ate the meager rations, and drank some water. He also used some water to wash the blood off his warhammer. After a while, Tal returned with a companion for Kala. She was kept blindfolded until she was in the hidden chamber.

Tal said, "Take off the blindfold after I leave."

Kala said, "Thank you. See you later." As Tal closed the secret door behind him.

Chapter 13

After waiting patiently for what felt like an eternity, the potioneer finally returned to her quaint little shop. As she opened the door, she was met with the eager faces of four men who had been waiting outside. A warm smile adorned her lips as she invited them in, leaving the door ajar, as if extending an open invitation to her potion-filled haven. The moment they stepped inside, their eyes widened with awe at the sight that greeted them. The shop was a vision of pristine cleanliness, with every potion neatly organized on labeled shelves according to size and type.

Bevin wasted no time in getting to the point, his curiosity piqued by the variety of healing potions on offer. "What are the prices for the different types of healing potions?" he inquired, eager to know the cost of their potential salvation.

Natasha, with an air of confidence, responded promptly, "Common healing potions are priced at fifty gold pieces, greater healing potions cost one hundred gold, and supreme healing potions come at five hundred. But if you're after something more unique, we can discuss the specifics, though specialty healings start at twelve hundred gold pieces. Just bear in mind, I'll need the necessary components and ample time to concoct the perfect potion for you."

Grinning with satisfaction, Bevin thanked her, aware that his companions were eagerly seeking their own remedies. Natasha's smile softened with a hint of amusement, and she playfully rolled her eyes. "As long as they have the gold, I'll have just what they need," she quipped, the light banter revealing her no-nonsense attitude.

Rashe leaned in and whispered, "Looks like she knows you're not one to carry much gold, my friend."

Bevin chuckled in response, his voice barely above a whisper, "Well, she can smell poverty, it seems."

Meanwhile, Adran made his intentions clear, listing the potions he sought to purchase. Natasha swiftly calculated the sum and informed him, "That'll be one thousand gold pieces, including the poison antidote."

Handing over the coins with an awkward smile, Adran thanked her and received his requested potions. Yet, Natasha couldn't help but tease, "If that's your flirting smile, you might want to work on it a bit." A playful wink accompanied her words as she handed him the vials.

Rashe couldn't help himself but chuckle at his friend's lack of charm but also knew that Adran's true worth lay in his unwavering loyalty and friendship. After securing his own potions, Rashe turned and joined the others, feeling grateful for their bond.

Next, Morros approached Natasha with a different request, seeking a potion of invisibility. Natasha replied, "I can brew it for you, but I'll need time to gather the components. How soon do you require it?"

Morros, with no pressing deadline, replied, "No rush, but how long will you need?"

"Around three days," Natasha informed him with certainty.

Content with the timeline, Morros agreed, "I'll be back in three days to pick it up. And what'll be the total cost?"

"Two thousand five hundred gold, with half as a deposit," she informed him matter-of-factly.

Placing one thousand five hundred gold pieces on the counter, Morros nodded and rejoined his companions outside the shop. Their pockets now considerably lighter, they turned back to the tavern, where an unexpected scene awaited them.

Gazing upon the commotion outside the tavern, the group hesitated to approach the city guards and the gathering crowd. Ranala, standing across the street, seemed to hold some insight into the situation, so Rashe approached her, seeking answers.

"What happened here?" he inquired with genuine concern.

Ranala's eyes reflected the gravity of the situation as she explained, "A mysterious dwarf, never before seen, entered the tavern and attacked three elves without any provocation. He vanished into thin air before the guard could catch him."

Rashe's mind quickly assessed the possibilities, "Do you think someone helped him escape?"

"Wouldn't be the first time," Ranala affirmed, leaving them with a lingering sense of intrigue as they pondered the events that had unfolded.

Rashe returned to his companions, recounting the details of her conversation with Tal. As they stood amidst the bustling commotion, a mysterious hooded figure approached them. It was none other than the enigmatic human who had been distributing jobs and payments at the booth.

The hooded elf introduced himself as Tal, his gaze fixed on the group. "I don't know you, but from the description of your group, you must be Kaz's friends. I am Tal, and if you are the group I think you are, I have work for you," he stated cryptically.

Bevin stepped forward, introducing himself, "I am Bevin, and yes, Kaz is our friend."

The rest of the group turned to look at Tal, and he said, "Let's move away from all this to where we can talk."

The party followed Tal down the street a bit, and when they were out of sight of the guard and crowd, he stopped to talk to them.

The hooded human looked at them and said, "I am Tal of Kuccivis, and people of this area entrust me to find them help from time to time. Kaz talked to me a few days ago and said he had a group that would be more than suitable for the work I have to be done."

Bevin replied, "Well met Tal of Kuccivis. What work do you have for us?"

Tal said, "I have a contract that was not spoken for, and it could be a good way for you and your friends to prove your worth."

Bevin said, "What needs to be done?"

Tal explained, "One of the local merchants has a special package that needs to be safely delivered to a customer, and he fears that some bandits are waiting to intercept the delivery. He wants to ensure that the delivery gets made and needs confirmation of delivery by obtaining the customer's seal once the package got delivered and returning that confirmation to me."

Bevin said, "Seems easy enough. Where do we obtain the package, and where does it need to be delivered?"

Tal pulled out a small box and said, "Here's the package, and it needs to be delivered to Jaral Haunthnor at the crossroads at the southwestern base of The Crags no later than three days from tomorrow."

Bevin said, "How far was the Crags, and how will we find Jaral?"

Tal replied, "Head east out of town for three days, and you will find the crossroads. Jaral will be looking for you, and the box will let him know you are near."

Bevin said, "We shall leave at once and return as soon as we have received the seal of Jaral Haunthnor."

Tal said, "There's another matter that needs special attention also."

Bevin replies, "Two jobs in one. There must be some good pay on this."

Tal said, "There was. The second job will require some finesse, coordination, and discretion."

Morros said, "Sounds like something of my specialties."

Tal looked at Morros and said, "There's an individual that needs to get out of town under cover of darkness."

Morros said, "Sounds like someone that maybe the guard was looking for."

Tal replied, "I have a friend that will be ready with an airship tonight at midnight. Meet him on the ship, and I will ensure the individual meets you there. You can use the airship to make your delivery also; be ready for anything."

Adran looked at Rashe and said, "Sounds like we have an interesting night in store for us."

Tal said, "See you at midnight on the airship." And he disappeared into the shadows.

Tal made his way to where the airship was docked to speak with Sylv, the airship's captain. Tal knows that Sylv was a very skilled captain and a good fit to work with this group of Kaz's friends. He knows that he needs to find his price to fly so late when the sky could be filled with dragons or wyverns.

Tal approached and said, "Sylv, my friend, how are you today?"

Sylv replied, "It was a great day until you showed up."

Tal said, "I have your fifty gold pieces here for the last jo……"

Sylv cut him off, "shut your mouth and come aboard."

Sylv takes the coin as Tal boards the airship and whispers, "keep your voice down and get out of here."

Tal said, "Was that any way to greet a friend that brings you a way to make a lot of gold."

Sylv snarled and said, "Last job almost cost me my piloting job, and fifty gold will not replace that!"

Tal said, "My friend Kaz has some friends that need to make a delivery of a rare object only three days from here. I can pay you three times the last job, and this time all you have to do was get them there and back."

Sylv said, "It's never easy when you are involved."

Tal replied, "This time it was. They need a ride to the crossroads to deliver and come back here. That was all."

Sylv looked at him intently and tried to gain an accurate read on how truthful he was, and asked, "how many passengers and how much cargo?"

Tal smiled at him and said, "Four passengers and one crate."

Sylv said, "five hundred gold and pay half up front."

Tal said, "Two hundred and fifty and fifty paid up front."

Sylv said, "Five hundred, pay two fifty up front, and I don't talk to the city guard speaking to the dock master right now."

Tal looked at the guard and said, "Here, two hundred and fifty gold. See you at midnight tonight." And he left the airship and slipped away in the shadows.

Sylv said to himself, "Midnight? I should have doubled it for that late of a flight."

The city guard approached the airship Sylv was on and said, "Can we check your ship for any stowaways? We are looking for a murderer."

Sylv replied, "Please come aboard. I would hate to think there was a murderer on the loose and hiding on the ship I captain."

The guard replied, "thank you. It shouldn't take long. You have not seen any unusual people about, have you?"

Sylv chuckled and said, "Unusual people in Frostwood Haven? Well, none that I have not seen before."

The guard seemed less than amused but laughed and said, "We do have some unusual people here. More now that the Tainted Rose arrived on its annual trip."

Sylv replied, "The Tainted Rose always seems to bring the strangest of passengers."

The guard finished its search and said, "No other holds or hides on this ship, are there?"

Sylv said, "No sir that was it."

The guard said, "Alert the guard if you see anyone. There will be extra guards on patrol tonight."

Sylv said, "Good to know. Hate to think some murderer was hiding out here in Frostwood

Haven."

The guard looked at him, unsure if he was

Chapter 14

T al enters the hidden room and calls out, "Kala, I am back and need to talk to you."

Kala replies, "Be right out." And steps from the back room in his regular clothing.

Tal says, "Your companion should leave now."

The dwarven female stepped into the room, and Tal placed the blindfold back on her. He opened the door and walked her safely down the street, turned a few times, and kept to the shadows to ensure she was properly confused about the location. Once he had thoroughly confused her, he stopped and removed the blindfold. Tal handed her a pouch of gold and silver coins, then walked away in a different direction than where they had come from. Once again, ensuring that he had not been followed or seen going into the alley, he waited a few minutes, then opened the secret door and slipped inside. Kala was sitting at the small table and munching on some stale crackers.

Tal said, "Tonight, I will be coming back with a

wagon and a crate to get you out of town,"

Kala replied, "how far will I have to ride in the crate, and won't the city guard be searching wagons on the road tonight?"

Tal explained, "You will get into the crate, and we will travel the roads that the guards have been paid off on. That road leads to the airship landing area, and there was an airship waiting for you to be loaded on."

Kala said, "So I am to be cargo?"

Tal said, "Just until we are out of the city, you can get out of the crate. The group you will be traveling with will be ready to help you, and they may require your skills where they are going."

Kala replied, "I am not happy about sitting in a box, but if it gets me out of going to the city dungeon for killing those damn elves, then I am in."

Tal chuckled, "a good choice, my friend. I will leave after sundown, since people expect me, and return with the cart before midnight. The airship captain and the others will await our arrival at midnight."

Kala said, "Any chance I could get some decent food and drink before that?"

Tal replied, "I will do my best to bring you something. There are a lot of guards searching everywhere, and we cannot take the risk of being discovered."

Tal took a seat at the small table and shortly fell asleep sitting there. He knew that if he napped in a chair, he would only sleep briefly. In the short time that Tal slept, Kala cleaned his warhammer, put on his armor, and prepared to become cargo. Tal fell from his chair and startled himself awake as he hit the ground.

Kala chuckled, "time to get up!"

Tal looked at him and asked, "How long did I sleep?"

Kala replied, "Just a short rest. There's still time before we have to meet the airship."

Tal said, "Maybe enough time to go get the cart and crate, but not enough to get you a good meal now. Should have woken me earlier to fill that belly of yours."

Kala said, "Anything you could bring more than these stale crackers and dry fruit would be fine with me."

As Tal was getting off the ground, he said, "If there was time, but most importantly, we have to be on time for the airship."

Kala grumbled, "I guess I will get my fill on what was here while you head out."

Tal looked at him, shook his head, and headed out the secret door. He looked about to ensure no one was around to see him, and he crept out into the darkness of the night. He made his way down the side streets until he reached Marask's workshop and took a good long look around to ensure there were no guards nearby. Once it was clear, he moved across the street and into the back door. After he got inside, he saw a horse hitched to a wagon with a large crate loaded on it, but Marask was nowhere to be found. As he moved up the side of the wagon, he saw a note attached to it that read, "Return the cart and horse in the morning." Tal opened the doors and led the horse out of the workshop. He closed the workshop, got in the cart, and headed back to get Kala. As Tal headed down the streets, a guard patrol stopped him.

The guard said, "pretty late to be making a delivery."

Tal said, "That's just an empty crate I am returning to my store so I can use it again. It saves me gold to empty the delivery and reuse the crates."

The guard eyed him and asked, "Mind if we open it then?"

Tal replied, "Not at all. I can open it for you if you like."

The guard unsheathed their swords and said, "Open it slowly."

Tal moved slowly and said, "I promise it's empty." He opened the crate to show it was empty.

The guard looked inside the crate and said,

"Looks like Marask's woodworking."

Tal replied, "Best woodworker in the city."

The guard said, "Be on your way. Keep an eye out and alert the guard if you see anything suspicious."

Tal said, "I will. Have a good night." He closed up the crate and continued down the road.

While Tal was preparing his plan to get Kala to the airship, the rest of the party was making their way to the airship. The streets of Frostwood Haven were filled with city guards, and every person was being looked at as a suspect. If a dwarf was walking down the street, they were questioned, especially if they were carrying a warhammer. The Fortuitous Few were not questioned as suspects but were looked at since they were somewhat new to Frostwood Haven. This, of course, did make them uncomfortable since they were going to be helping the dwarf escape and were concerned about being followed and watched too closely.

Morros said, "Being new in Frostwood Haven makes it harder to blend in with a killer being searched for."

Rashe replied, "Hard to keep that low profile that Kaz wanted us to keep."

Bevin stated, "as long as we do not have a dwarf with us or be seen with one, we should be just fine."

Adran chuckled, "Hopefully, that's not the second city we cannot return to."

Rashe looked at him and retorted, "Nothing like bringing on a bit of bad luck, my friend."

Adran countered, "Someone once said skill was better than luck since luck was something you create yourself."

Rashe smiled and replied, "You do listen when I talk."

Adran laughed, "Only when you say things worth listening to."

All four of them laughed and continued down the street. They made a short stop at the street market again to purchase fresh fruits and look at what else was available. There were several vendors selling goods and trinkets. Most of the items in the market were things that the party had no use for, and they just continued to walk around. While walking around, Morros wandered off from the party and began to look at fabrics that were for sale. The young lady selling the fabric was busy talking with a customer while he fingered the fabrics and occasionally looked up to catch her eye. This was the same tiefling female he had seen before. She finished up selling several yards of fabric to her customer and turned to look at Morros.

She said, "Can I help you find something for your wife?"

Morros replied, "I have no wife, and I was just considering some fabric for a new set of clothing."

She said, "Well, that translucent red silk would make a very fine suit. It may show off more than you would want to show in public though."

Morros chuckled and said, "What do you recommend…..I'm sorry I did not introduce myself. I am Morros, and you are?"

She replied, "I am Madrin, and I would recommend you seek cloth from a tailor instead of my fabrics that are for dresses and gowns."

Morros smiled and said, "If I find a good tailor, I will need a reason to have some fine clothes made. Maybe we could meet again in a week and find a reason to wear fine clothing."

Madrin smiled and replied, "I guess if I am here in a week you will know my answer."

Bevin called out, "we need to move on Morros."

Morros glanced at Bevin, then back at Madrin, and said, "I will see you in a week when I return to Frostwood Haven."

Madrin smiled and said, "We shall see."

Morros walked off and rejoined his companions as they made their way out of the town square. Morros glanced over his shoulder and caught Madrin's stare as she smiled and turned her head. Bevin slapped Morros on the back, smiled at him, and chuckled. Each of the friends laughed and smiled at Morros as he gave them all a toothy infernal grin.

Rashe egged on the laughter, commenting, "Leave

it to Morros the charismatic to find the one female tiefling in Frostwood Haven and dazzle her in less than a minute."

Adran interjected, "hopefully, when they meet again, it was not less than a minute."

They all laughed at Morros' expense, including Morros, and continued to go board the airship.

As Tal prepared to deliver special cargo the Fortuitous few boarded the ship. Sylv was standing on the main deck waiting for their arrival and working on the navigational charts. He seemed very preoccupied and did not notice the crew come aboard. They watched as he made notes on the charts and used some apparatus to look up into the sky and seem to take some measurements. He also took some time to look at another instrument with some sort of spinning spoons on top of it. After each time he looked at the strange apparatus he would make notes on the charts and another piece of parchment in front of him. After a few minutes of watching him he just stared at the map in front of him like he was in a trance of some kind.

Adran said, "Hello captain. At least I am assuming you are the captain."

Sylv looked up and was startled by the interruption and said, "Yes, I am the captain. What can I do for you?"

Adran replied, "We are the ones that were sent by

Kaz and Tal."

Sylv said, "You don't look like an airship crew."

Bevin said, "We have worked many jobs, but an airship crew was new for us."

Sylv chuckled, "well, I guess with this special cargo, a specific set of skills are in need."

Rashe said, "Yes, we each have a very specific set of skills that seem to fit a multitude of jobs in different areas."

Morros said, "Some skills we still have yet to explore."

Sylv said, "Well, this time, you get to explore your skills aboard an airship. I will go over all that needs to be done during takeoff, sky sailing, and landing. While we go over these things, we will find what fits best for each of you. I am Sylv, by the way. What are your names, and have you had any experience on flying or sailing ships?"

Adran introduced himself and said, "I have sailed before, but it has been some time since I did it last."

Bevin said, "I am Bevin Fengala, and I have sailed only as a passenger."

Morros said, "I am Morros, and I have no experience with ships other than riding in them."

Rashe responds, "I am Rashe, and I am assuming that music will not involved in any of this?"

Sylv chuckled and said, "a small bit of musical talent can help if you can blow the boatswain's whistle."

Rashe said, "If you have one, I will give it a go."

Sylv said, "There was one near the wheel, and I can show you how to use it once everyone was more settled."

Rashe replied, "I will meet you near the wheel, and I will have a look at the whistle while I wait."

Sylv leads the new temporary crew around and shows them how to bring in the ropes, store them, and prepare the sails. Luckily this was a smaller vessel and only requires two people to bring in the ropes, one to ready the sails, and the captain to navigate lifting off. Once the jobs were described and demonstrated, Sylv gave out the assignments. Adran and Morros will bring in the ropes, Bevin will set the sails, and Rashe will be with the captain sounding the calls on the boatswain's whistle. Rashe practiced the different calls as each other member practiced their new position. Rashe blew a low-pitched whistle that quickly went to a high-pitched whistle to signal haul in the lines and a solid high pitch whistle to hold the line and pause. He blew a low-pitched whistle that rose to a high-pitched whistle to raise the sails and a high-pitched whistle that turned low to lower the sails.

Once each member was comfortable enough to do their assigned duty skillfully enough to convince someone they were actual crew members, they took a break for dinner. Rashe piped a melody of low to high tones on the boatswain's whistle to sound dinner for the crew after Bevin had gone into the galley to prepare a meal for them all. The captain and his new crew members sat at a rectangular table filled with meat, green vegetables, and boiled potatoes. The captain was sitting at the head of the table, and each of the four new crew members sat along the sides, two on each side. The captain looked at the meal on the table and smiled, then looked at Bevin with an approving smile and nod of his head.

Sylv said, "Quite the meal you have prepared us. A fine meal to celebrate a good day of quick learning and no injuries."

Bevin replied, "Only a skilled teacher could yield the results of good learning."

Morros said, "I would like to learn how to fly this airship and maybe own one of my own one day."

Rashe said, "It sure beats walking or riding a horse everywhere."

Adran said, "If you buy one, we will have to build a new docking area in Hoskavek."

Morros said, "That would be the simple part. We would have to clear trees to be able to fly into Hoskavek."

Bevin countered, "No cutting the trees down. We must consult the Oak Father for his help and guidance if you want to move them."

Sylv stated, "the first problem would be getting enough gold to buy an airship."

Morros looked at Sylv, smiled, and said, "I am sure we could negotiate with someone to come up with a fair price."

Sylv retorted, "I only drive this one and others. I do not own one."

Morros said, "I am sure you know who we could speak with, and wouldn't you like to be your own captain instead of someone's employee?"

Sylv gave a puzzled look and said, "That would be nice, but if I am flying your airship would I not still be an employee?"

Morros replied, "A member of the group, not an employee. Of course, we need to see how this job goes and if you are a good fit with us and if you would be interested in joining up with us."

Sylv said, "I guess we will see what comes from delivering this special cargo."

They all felt tired as they ate, spoke amongst each other, and cleaned the galley. It had already been a long day, and it would be longer once midnight came. Since they had an hour or so before sundown and several hours before midnight, they decided to get some rest and be refreshed before their cargo arrived and the journey began. Sylv had shown them before where the crew's quarters were, and each of them retreated there, chose a bunk, and took a rest. They set watches so that one of the four was always awake, which ensured they would not oversleep. This also ensured that when the city guard made their rounds, they would be less interested in coming aboard since a watch was always posted on the ship. As midnight began to approach the party and the captain were awake and awaiting the arrival of their cargo.

On the other side of town Tal went down the back road toward his hidden room, he looked about to ensure nobody was around. When he knew the area was clear, he backed the horse and cart into the alley near the hidden door. He parked the cart and opened up the crate. He then jumped down off the cart and opened the secret door. He looked in and saw that Kala was waiting for his arrival and ready to move. Without a word from either of them, Kala exited the door, jumped into the cart, and sat down in the crate. Tal closed it up behind him and began to drive towards the airship landing area.

Tal had his route mapped out in his head and made his way down the roads that he knew the guards, and they were already paid to look the other way. Tal made it a habit to keep some of the city guards paid better than their monthly wage just for times like this. He knew the ones he could trust to take the payments since he either had something on them or they needed the money for a large family. One guard was paid exceptionally well since he was one of the patrol leaders, and he had six children at home with another on the way. It just happened that this guard oversaw the patrol on the road to the airship landing field and the landing area. The guard on the road stopped him and made it look like they searched his cargo, then sent him on his way. Upon arriving at the airship landing area, the patrol leader and the guard at the entrance were not whom he was expecting.

The guard yelled, "HALT!"

Tal pulled the reins and replied, "Yes sir. How are you this fine night?"

The guard looked at him and said, "This was a very late delivery. What are you carrying?"

Tal said, "A crate to be delivered to the artificer's guild in Mirabar. I was told it was dangerous. So, we decided to move it late at night so no people would be in danger if something happened."

The guard looked at him quizzically and asked, "What kind of dangerous?"

Tal replied, "I don't know much about it, but I was told if it were to fall or shake too much, it would be like a breath from a dragon."

The patrol leader and guard stepped back and asked, "Could you open it and show us what it contains?"

Tal stood up and said, "Let me get my crowbar and yank the side off."

The patrol leader said, "No, no, no. You just keep on moving slowly, and we will watch you from here."

Tal sat back down and said, "It's no trouble. I am sure it would not jar it too much if I pried the side open. I mean, how else will the artificers open it?"

The patrol leader barks, "Just move on and get it loaded so it can leave here as quickly as possible."

Tal responded, "Okay, then should I tell the airship captain to go ahead and fly tonight instead of waiting for the morning?"

The patrol leader answered, "Yes, the faster he gets this out of the city, the better."

Tal reined his horse and said, "That does sound like the best thing to do. Good night."

As he slowly moved the cart away from the guard, he turned towards the awaiting airship and the new crew that had boarded earlier. Tal pulled the cart past the gangplank to the airship, and the crew unloaded the crate and carefully carried it up to the main deck. Then, they slowly lowered it into the cargo hold as Tal loudly explained that the patrol leader permitted them to lift off as soon as possible. Tal disembarked from the ship, and the crew prepared to lift off into the midnight sky.

Rashe sounded his boatswain's whistle signaling Adran and Morros to bring in the lines, then sounding the alert for Bevin to raise the sails. Once all the lines were in and the sails full the airship lifted off and Sylv skillfully piloted them into the night sky.

Chapter 15

A s the magnificent airship gracefully lifted off the ground, it seemed to dance with the stars in the velvety night sky. The crew gazed in wonderment, their eyes tracing the twinkling constellations that seemed to draw nearer with each passing moment. The night air enveloped them in a gentle embrace, carrying the promise of an otherworldly journey. As they ascended higher and higher, the temperature dropped, and a crisp, refreshing chill settled around them, tingling their skin like a lover's gentle caress.

Above, the celestial canvas unfurled its grand spectacle, adorned with an array of stars that glowed like shimmering diamonds against the dark tapestry of space. The few wisps of clouds scattered about seemed to only enhance the brilliance, creating a magical effect as if the heavens themselves had prepared this celestial symphony for their exclusive delight. The full moon, radiant and luminous, beamed down upon them, casting an ethereal glow that illuminated the airship's deck, bathing the crew in a soft, silvery light.

The enchantment of the night sky captivated every heart on board, except for Elaina, who, rather than gazing upward, fixated on Sylv. She observed his face, transformed by the celestial beauty, and couldn't help but be drawn to his sense of wonder. For Sylv, this night flight was unlike any other experience he had known before; it was a celestial rendezvous that evoked the innocence and awe of his very first time in the air.

With every passing moment, the airship climbed higher, and the stars seemed to wink playfully at them, sharing in the secrets of the universe. Time itself appeared to slow, allowing the crew to savor every fleeting second of this extraordinary night flight. The air held a serene stillness, broken only by the soft hum of the airship's engines, like a tender whisper in the ears of lovers.

As they reached the zenith of their ascent, Sylv skillfully leveled off the airship, and with a gentle touch, set its course toward their destination. The stars now spread across the sky like an endless ocean, guiding their path as celestial navigators. Each member of the crew found themselves wrapped in a surreal dreamscape, where reality merged with fantasy, and the very notion of time lost its grip.

In the distance, a shooting star streaked across the heavens, leaving a trail of stardust in its wake, as if to bless their nocturnal voyage. Sylv felt an inexplicable connection to the night sky, as if the very essence of flight was entwined with the mystical allure of the stars. In this ethereal realm, he reveled in the embrace of the night, cherishing every passing moment as if it were a cherished memory.

As the airship finally cleared the view of the city, a tense silence settled over the crew. The time had come to open the shipping crate that contained Kala, their unexpected passenger. The atmosphere was thick with discomfort as the crew exchanged uneasy glances, unsure of what to expect. Before the crate was even pried open, the air was heavy with palpable tension.

Sylv, his voice strained, turned to Kala and began to speak, his words carefully measured. "Listen up, Kala," he began, his tone firm. "We've got elves onboard this ship, and they ain't your enemies. We're all in the same boat here, and we need to work together if we're gonna make it through this."

Kala's grip on his warhammer tightened, his eyes narrowing as he stared at Sylv and the crew. Suspicion hung thick in the air, and his response was laden with a guarded wariness.

"I've heard plenty of promises before," he retorted, his voice edged with skepticism. "But actions speak louder than words."

The tension grew as the crew gathered around the crate, their hands resting on their weapons, eyes never leaving Kala. With a slow, deliberate motion, the lid of the crate was lifted, revealing Kala's tense form within. His muscles coiled like a tightly wound spring, ready to unleash his warhammer at the slightest hint of threat.

As the crate creaked open, Kala's gaze darted from face to face, his expression a mix of caution and defiance. The crew mirrored his wariness, their own discomfort evident in their stiff postures and steely gazes. Each member of the airship held their breath, the air thick with a sense of unease.

With measured steps, Kala emerged from the crate, his warhammer held aloft and his stance defensive. The crew, equally on edge, maintained a wary distance, their hands poised to draw their weapons if necessary. Kala's introduction was curt and cautious, his words chosen with care. "Name's Kala," he stated, his voice low and steady. "Don't take my presence as some sort of trust pact."

The crew exchanged uneasy glances, the

strained atmosphere underscoring their introductions. Each word was measured, each movement calculated, as they navigated the delicate dance of unfamiliarity and mistrust. The airship, once a bastion of camaraderie, was now a vessel of tension and uncertainty.

As Kala's warhammer clanged against the airship's wooden floor, the sound echoed like a lingering reminder of the unease that pervaded the scene. The crew, though physically together, remained emotionally divided, their unspoken thoughts and lingering doubts casting a shadow over the introductions. In this moment, the airship felt like a fragile bubble, teetering on the precipice of conflict or cooperation, with Kala's presence as the catalyst that could tip the balance in either direction.

And so, the airship glided through the night, an elegant dance partner among the constellations, harmonizing with the cosmos. The crew, united by the enchantment of the night, embraced this shared experience as something truly magical. In the dark embrace of the heavens, they were not mere travelers but ethereal beings, drawn by the allure of the night sky's celestial symphony.

As the night descended, and the stars began to shimmer in the dark sky, the airship was now ready for its late-night flight. Among the passengers waiting onboard was Elaina, a striking and mysterious woman seeking safe passage out of the North. Her captivating silver eyes sparkled like moonlit waters, and her long flowing hair cascaded like a waterfall of midnight. Elaina had an air of elegance and grace, but a certain sadness lurked behind her enchanting gaze.

From the moment she boarded the airship, Elaina couldn't help but be captivated by Sylv, the seasoned captain. His rugged charm, coupled with his confident command of the ship, intrigued her deeply. The way he moved with grace and precision, his firm voice calling out orders, only heightened her admiration for the skilled pilot.

Throughout the journey, Elaina found herself stealing glances at Sylv whenever she thought he wasn't looking. Her heart would flutter whenever their eyes met, and she'd quickly avert her gaze, hoping her infatuation remained hidden. She admired his dedication to ensuring the safety of his passengers and marveled at the way he expertly navigated the skies.

As the airship glided through the night, Elaina couldn't help but wonder about the events that had led her to this moment. What secrets and burdens did she carry that compelled her to seek refuge in the far reaches of the world?

Her mind drifted back to Sylv, imagining a future where she could be by his side, soaring through the skies together, free from the shadows of her past. But she knew that such dreams were but fleeting illusions.

Elaina struggled to find the courage to speak to Sylv, to share her story and seek solace in his company. Yet, every time she approached him, her heart would race, and her words would falter. The fear of rejection and the weight of her past kept her silent.

Unknown to Elaina, Sylv had noticed her stealing glances at him throughout the journey. Although he remained focused on piloting the airship, her presence had not gone unnoticed. He found her intriguing and sensed that there was more to her than met the eye.

As the journey progressed, Elaina's infatuation with Sylv grew stronger, and she felt an undeniable pull towards him. She longed to break free from the confines of her emotions and share her feelings with him, but the fear of vulnerability held her back.

The night air whispered its secrets as the airship soared through the darkness. Elaina's heart yearned to open up to Sylv, to find comfort and acceptance in his presence. Yet, she hesitated, unsure if she was ready to confront her past and embrace the future.

Little did she know that the night held many surprises, and perhaps the stars themselves would conspire to bring their paths together? As the airship continued on its journey, Elaina's feelings for Sylv remained like stars sparkling in the vast expanse of her heart, waiting for the right moment to shine bright.

And so, amidst the enchanting spectacle of the night sky, Sylv steered the airship on its celestial dance, while Elaina's heart danced in harmony with her infatuation, a delicate rhythm woven into the tapestry of this mystical night journey. In this shared moment between the heavens and mortal souls, the destinies of the airship, its crew, and Elaina entwined, guided by the stars that glimmered like beacons of hope in the vast expanse of the universe. The night had secrets to reveal, and the airship, with Sylv at the helm, was ready to embrace the mysteries that awaited them in the darkness beyond.

Chapter 16

Elaina had a background marked by tragedy, danger, and a daring escape from enslavement. Born into a humble family in a small village, she led a peaceful and content life until a group of ruthless raiders, followers of Hodur, descended upon her home. The marauders showed no mercy, leaving devastation in their wake. They kidnapped and enslaved Elania after killing her parents.

For years, Elaina endured the harsh and oppressive life of a slave, her spirit nearly broken by the cruelty of her captors. Forced to toil endlessly in grueling conditions, she witnessed the suffering of her fellow slaves and the endless torment inflicted upon them. Yet, a flicker of resilience remained within her, a glimmer of hope that refused to be extinguished.

One fateful night, during a violent storm that raged over the slavers' camp, an opportunity for escape presented itself. Elania's heart pounded in her chest as she darted through the pelting rain, every drop a reminder of the cruel lashings she had endured at the hands of the cult. The storm's fury mirrored her own, a tempest of emotions driving her forward. Her limbs were heavy with exhaustion, but the adrenaline coursing through her veins kept her moving, fueled by the burning desire to break free from the chains that had bound her for far too long.

The rain-soaked ground squelched beneath her feet, and the trees above creaked in protest, their branches swaying dangerously in the violent winds. The deafening roar of thunder masked the sound of her frantic footsteps, and the flashes of lightning provided fleeting glimpses of the treacherous path ahead.

She knew that her escape had to be swift and silent. Any wrong move, any misstep, and she would be dragged back into the clutches of the cult. The storm offered both an advantage and a risk; it concealed her movements but also threatened to betray her to the relentless pursuit of the slavers.

As she pushed forward, the storm grew more ferocious, and the heavens opened up, unleashing a torrential downpour that transformed the camp into a quagmire of mud and chaos. The cult members scrambled to secure their belongings and protect their torches from the relentless rain.

Elania seized this moment of confusion and

disarray to slip past the oblivious guards, her heart racing in her throat. She navigated through the maze of tents and crude structures, her mind working with the precision of a seasoned escape artist. She knew that the cult's leader, a sinister figure who reveled in the torment of the enslaved, would not rest until she was hunted down.

With every step, she pushed herself harder, urging her weary body onward. The storm seemed to whip her forward, as if nature itself were guiding her towards freedom. The rain soaked through her tattered clothes, chilling her to the bone, but she pressed on, fueled by the determination to reclaim her stolen life.

As she neared the outskirts of the camp, she spotted a flash of movement through the trees. Fear gripped her heart, but as she looked closer, she realized that it was not a pursuer. Instead, a flash flood was rapidly forming, the rainwater collecting in the low-lying areas and surging towards the camp.

Elania's heart raced, and a flicker of hope ignited within her. The flash flood was nature's ally, a force that could divert the cult members' attention and provide a fleeting window for her escape. She knew she had to seize this opportunity. Swiftly changing her course, she directed her steps away from the flood's path, using the chaos of the storm to her advantage. The cult members, preoccupied with securing their camp, remained unaware of the danger approaching.

As the floodwaters swelled, a rush of relief washed over Elania. With the cult members scrambling to protect themselves from the sudden deluge, she could slip away unnoticed, like a shadow swallowed by the night. Her heart pounded with a mix of fear and hope as she traversed the treacherous terrain, making her way to higher ground. The rain continued to fall relentlessly, shrouding her escape in a cloak of secrecy. The floodwaters carried away the evidence of her presence, leaving the cult to believe that she had been washed away in the calamity.

As the storm gradually subsided, Elania found herself far from the confines of the slavers' camp. She had escaped the clutches of the cult, but her journey was far from over. The storm may have abated, but a tempest of emotions and challenges awaited her on the horizon. With her heart heavy with the weight of her past and her spirit ignited with the flames of freedom, Elania embarked on a treacherous quest to rebuild her life and find her place in a world that had once sought to extinguish her light.

Guided by an unyielding will and the resilience of her spirit, she vowed to reclaim her stolen identity, rising from the shadows of her past like a phoenix reborn from the ashes. The storm had gifted her a second chance, and she would embrace it, fiercely determined to forge her own destiny and become the master of her own fate.

Her escape led her to wander the treacherous landscapes of the North, seeking refuge in the most remote and unforgiving corners of the world. Each step she took was haunted by the memories of her past, pushing her onward in search of safety and solace. Along her journey, she faced danger from wild beasts, hostile tribes, and the ever-looming threat of being recaptured by the slavers.

Despite the perils, Elaina's determination and resourcefulness became her allies. She learned to survive, adapting to the harsh conditions and honing her skills in self-defense. Along the way, she encountered kind-hearted individuals who offered her shelter and guidance, providing a glimmer of light amidst the darkness that had shrouded her life.

Elaina's escape brought her to the city of Frost-wood Haven, where she hoped to find a means to leave the North and embark on a new chapter of her life. It was here that fate would lead her to cross paths with Sylv, the airship captain, and the night flight that would change her life forever.

In the presence of Sylv, Elaina found herself

drawn to his strength, kindness, and unwavering determination. His role as an airship captain awakened a yearning within her to embrace freedom in all its forms, soaring through the skies as untethered as the stars above. Yet, the shadows of her past still lingered, leaving her hesitant to reveal the depths of her journey and the trauma she had endured.

As the airship carried her toward an uncertain future, Elaina's heart yearned to share her story with Sylv, to find solace and understanding in his embrace. However, fear held her back, afraid of being judged or rejected, and uncertain if she could ever fully escape the shadows of her past.

Amidst the mesmerizing night sky, Elaina's journey of healing and self-discovery had only just begun. The stars that glittered above bore witness to her resilience, her courage, and the profound strength she carried within. In the enchanting dance of the airship among the constellations, Elaina felt a glimmer of hope that perhaps, in the celestial embrace of the night, she could find a new beginning and a chance to embrace the freedom she had fought so hard to attain.

Chapter 17

As the airship gracefully cruised through the ethereal darkness, Elaina found herself drawn to the edge of the deck, her eyes fixed on the horizon where the moon and stars converged. Her heart fluttered with a mix of excitement and trepidation, for she knew that this journey held the promise of new beginnings. The wind tousled her hair, and the soft caress of the night air felt like a gentle reminder of the freedom she had yearned for so long. In the presence of Sylv, the skilled captain who seemed as much a part of the airship as its sails and riggings, Elaina sensed a kinship that transcended the boundaries of mere acquaintance. His steadfast determination and sense of purpose ignited a fire within her, empowering her to face the shadows of her past with newfound courage. With each passing moment, she felt herself drawn further into the celestial dance of the night, the stars above becoming her guiding lights, illuminating the path to a future filled with infinite possibilities.

As the airship journeyed deeper into the vast expanse of the universe, Elaina knew that her life had forever changed, and the tapestry of fate was weaving a grand tale that only the stars themselves could foretell.

In the midst of Elaina's contemplation, the tranquility of the night was abruptly shattered by a series of piercing screeches that echoed through the air. She turned to see dark silhouettes soaring towards the airship, their wings casting eerie shadows on the deck. The flying beasts had found them, and their eyes glowed with malice, hungry for the taste of blood.

"Sylv, we've got incoming!" Elaina's voice sliced through the air, urgency and determination intertwining in her tone.

Sylv's eyes narrowed, fingers clenching the ship's wheel with a vice-like grip. "Hold on tight, everyone! Battle stations!" His command cut through the tension, setting the crew into motion.

Rashe, the charismatic bard, positioned himself near the prow, his lute's strings trembling under his skillful touch. Melodic notes spilled from his instrument, a harmony that resonated with the primal forces of nature. The music's soothing embrace momentarily calmed the chaos, but the approaching creatures remained undeterred.

In the shadows, Morros, the agile rogue assassin,

moved like a wraith, his form barely visible as he darted into action. Emerging at the airship's edge, moonlight danced off his twin daggers. His attack was swift, a whirlwind of lethal precision that claimed one of the beasts, yet more emerged to take its place.

Adran and Bevin held their ground back-to-back, their gazes locked on the encroaching danger. A shared nod between them marked the beginning of their harmonious rhythm. Adran's body pulsed with ethereal energy, and a single punch sent a shockwave rippling through the air. Bevin's staff spun in a protective dance, fending off the relentless onslaught.

Elaina's breath steadied as unfamiliar magic coursed through her veins. She stretched her hand out, a cascade of stars responding to her call, swirling in a celestial vortex around her. With a determined thrust, she launched the stars toward the creatures, igniting upon impact and forcing a temporary retreat.

Sylv navigated the airship with finesse, evading the creatures' lunges with calculated grace. His gaze flickered to Elaina, conveying both trust and reliance. "Elaina, keep them at bay! I'll take us higher!" His voice cut through the chaos, anchoring her focus.

Elaina's resolve deepened. She channeled her

power, summoning more stars to shower down upon the attackers. The air around her hummed with celestial energy, her eyes ablaze with an otherworldly radiance.

Kala, his warhammer in hand, emerged from the shadows, his movements calculated and defensive. He joined the fray, his every strike ringing with a thunderous determination. His warhammer collided with the creatures' hardened scales, each blow punctuating his resilience.

Rashe's melody crescendoed, infusing the crew with renewed strength. His voice sang of courage and defiance, stoking the fire of determination that burned within each member.

Adran and Bevin's connection deepened as their movements synchronized flawlessly. Strikes resonated with unmatched precision, their combined force causing the creatures to falter and stagger.

Elaina's starry storm intensified, cascading over the remaining foes in a radiant explosion of light. Wings faltered, and the creatures retreated, acknowledging the indomitable force before them.

"We're pushing them back!" Elaina's triumphant cry echoed through the battle-torn air.

Sylv guided the airship higher, away from the dwindling threat. The creatures' pursuit waned, vanishing into the inky depths from which they emerged.

A collective cheer erupted from the crew, Rashe's grin as bright as the moon above. Morros cleaned his daggers, a glint of satisfaction gleaming in his eyes. "A fight well-fought," he remarked.

Adran and Bevin exchanged a silent nod, an unspoken acknowledgment of their seamless teamwork.

As the airship soared through the night, Elaina's heart swelled with a newfound sense of purpose. Her arcane power, Kala's unwavering strength, and the crew's unity had proven unbreakable. Above, the stars shone as a testament to their triumph, guiding them toward the horizon of endless possibilities.

The tapestry of destiny unfurled, its threads weaving a path through uncertainty. With their united spirits, the crew embraced the challenges ahead, knowing that the bonds they shared would carry them through the unknown. The universe itself seemed to applaud their courage, its infinite expanse a canvas awaiting their indelible mark.

Chapter 18

As the night sky gradually surrendered to the warm embrace of dawn, the Fortuitous Few roused from their slumber, greeted by the soft caress of the wind and the gentle promise of a new day. Elania, her eyes carrying the traces of a night spent wrapped in Sylv's presence, embarked on her morning ritual. The scent of freshly brewed coffee wafted through the air, mingling with the tantalizing aroma of toast and jam. With deft hands and a heart weighed down by the blend of sweet anticipation and the ache of impending separation, she prepared a modest breakfast to nourish the souls of the weary travelers. Her determination to savor every fleeting moment with Sylv, a desperate attempt to etch his image into her memory, painted her heart with a bittersweet symphony of emotions – a melodic dance of agony, joy, and the unquenchable thirst for more.

The airship, an elegant vessel of dreams and possibilities, glided through the azure canvas of the sky, its graceful ascent punctuated by the rhythmic hum of the engines and the whispers of the wind. Elania's gaze, though tethered to her tasks, often strayed towards Sylv – a man whose mere presence ignited stars within her chest. His commanding posture at the helm, his hands guiding the ship with a blend of finesse and determination, painted a portrait of strength and confidence that Elania found irresistible. With each stolen glance, she felt the tapestry of her destiny shifting, weaving threads of adventure and promise that unfurled before her like an uncharted map.

As the Fortuitous Few shared stories and laughter, their bond deepened, solidified by the shared canvas of the morning sky. The hues of orange and pink painted a breathtaking tableau, a canvas that seemed to mirror the spectrum of emotions swirling within their hearts. Their camaraderie, a blend of kindred spirits and unique essences, cast a warm glow over the airship's deck, dispelling any remnants of weariness or doubt.

Within this cocoon of shared moments, Elania was acutely aware of the ephemeral nature of time. Each fleeting instant, each stolen glance, became an offering to the universe – a prayer of gratitude for the opportunity to exist in this moment alongside Sylv. Bittersweet and beautiful, their connection held an intensity that transcended the boundaries of mere acquaintances, forging an unspoken bond that danced between longing and the unadulterated thrill of newfound companionship.

The journey, a symphony of sights and sounds, offered more than physical travel. It was a voyage of souls, an odyssey that unearthed buried dreams and ignited dormant passions. As the day unfurled its pages, the Fortuitous Few shared fragments of their past, stories that wove the tapestry of their identities, and aspirations that kindled flames of hope within their chests. Elania listened with rapt attention, her heart resonating with the chorus of shared experiences. In these moments, the airship transformed into a sanctuary of authenticity, a vessel that carried not just bodies, but the collective essence of their dreams.

For Elania, the sky had become a metaphor for her heart – expansive and unexplored, holding the potential for both turbulence and tranquility. As the airship soared through the heavens, she marveled at the serendipity that had brought this eclectic ensemble of souls together. Their connection felt like a carefully orchestrated masterpiece, each note of their shared laughter, each beat of their united hearts contributing to the harmonious symphony of their journey.

With every passing mile, every shared tale, Elania's spirit bloomed like a rare flower, its petals unfurling to embrace the tender caress of the wind. The ephemeral nature of their time together only deepened her resolve to absorb every nuance, every moment, into the fabric of her being. She knew that their paths might diverge, but the memories forged in the crucible of this shared adventure would remain as vivid as the constellations that adorned the sky.

As the airship descended towards its destination, Elania's heart brimmed with a potent blend of emotions – gratitude, melancholy, and the invigorating rush of embracing the unknown. Sylv had become a brushstroke on the canvas of her life, a figure that had infused her existence with color, depth, and a newfound sense of purpose. The chapter they had begun together, filled with laughter, shared stories, and stolen glances, had left an indelible mark on her soul. With the sun's warm embrace on her skin, Elania looked towards the horizon, her heart ablaze with the knowledge that this was just the beginning of her epic journey – a journey woven with the threads of connection, painted with the hues of passion, and propelled by the winds of destiny.

As the airship's descent slowed, Elania's steps carried her to Sylv's side, her heart heavy with the weight of impending farewell. The serenity of the moment seemed to magnify the tenderness of their connection, wrapping them in a cocoon of shared moments and unspoken promises. She turned to him, her gaze searching the depths of his eyes, hoping to find the words that danced on the edge of her lips.

"Sylv," she began, her voice soft yet laced with a quiet resolve. "These past days… they've been like a dream. A beautiful, fleeting dream that I wish could stretch on forever."

Sylv's gaze met hers, a mirror reflecting her emotions, his eyes cradling a myriad of unspoken sentiments. "Elania," he replied, his voice carrying a gentle ache, "you've brought a light into my life that I didn't realize was missing. Our time together has been nothing short of magical, and I find myself hoping that the threads that have woven us together won't unravel with the passing of distance."

A wistful smile graced Elania's lips, a bittersweet acknowledgment of the truth in Sylv's words. "I share that hope," she admitted, her fingers reaching out to brush against his. "It's as if we've been caught in the embrace of fate, and now, as our paths diverge, I can't help but wonder if destiny will once again find a way to intertwine our lives."

Sylv's touch was a tender caress, a silent affirmation of their shared longing. "Perhaps the stars above will bear witness to our unspoken wishes," he mused, his gaze drifting upwards, where the first glimmers of twilight began to paint the canvas of the sky.

As the airship gently touched down, the Fortuitous Few began to gather their belongings, their
footsteps a symphony of both finality and new
beginnings. Elania turned to Sylv, her heart heavy
with a mixture of sadness and hope. "Sylv, I... I
don't know what the future holds, but I want you
to know that you've ignited a fire within me, a fire
that won't easily be extinguished."

Sylv's eyes held a depth of emotion that words
couldn't fully convey. "Elania," he murmured, his
voice a whisper carried by the wind, "know that
you've kindled that same fire within me. Our paths
may take us in different directions, but I'll carry the
memory of you with me, a beacon of light to guide
me through the challenges that lie ahead."

With a heavy sigh, Elania leaned into Sylv's
embrace, her head resting against his chest as
if seeking solace in the rhythm of his heartbeat.
"Promise me something," she implored, her voice
muffled by the fabric of his shirt.

"Anything," Sylv responded, his arms encircling
her in a protective embrace.

"Promise me that we'll keep the flame alive, even
when distance tries to quench it. Promise me
that we won't let time erase the connection we've
shared."

Sylv's fingers gently lifted her chin, his eyes

locking onto hers with an intensity that sent ripples through her soul. "I promise," he declared, his words carrying the weight of a sacred vow. "No matter where our paths lead us, no matter how much time passes, I will hold onto the memory of this journey, of you, and the hope that one day, fate will reunite us."

Tears glistened in Elania's eyes, a testament to the depth of their emotions. "Then I'll hold onto that promise as well," she whispered, her voice a fragile melody amidst the symphony of departure.

Their lips brushed against each other in a lingering kiss, a fusion of sorrow and longing, a testament to the unspoken words that hung in the air. As they reluctantly parted, Elania's fingers traced the contours of Sylv's face, committing his features to memory.

"Until we meet again, Sylv," she whispered, her voice a tender farewell.

Sylv's gaze held hers, a silent echo of her sentiment. "Until then, Elania. May the stars above watch over you."

And with that, their hands slipped from each other's grasp, the embrace of destiny releasing its hold. As Elania stepped away, her heart a mélange of emotions, she carried with her the echo of Sylv's promise, a promise that whispered of a future yet unwritten, a future where their paths might once again converge amidst the vast expanse of the universe.

Chapter 19

With the airship now safely nestled in a secluded alcove, the Fortuitous Few bid a bittersweet farewell to Elania. The sun's golden embrace cast a warm, nostalgic hue across the landscape, a poignant backdrop to their final moments together. Emotions were carried on the gentle breeze, mingling with the scent of earth and distant wildflowers. Each hug and whispered word held the weight of the journey they had shared.

"Remember the stars, Elania," Rashe's voice was soft, his eyes reflecting the constellations they had gazed upon together. "They'll guide you as they guided us."

Adran's gaze, usually enigmatic, held a touch of vulnerability. "You've added your light to ours, and that light will always shine."

Bevin's smile was tinged with a hint of sadness. "May your path be as beautiful and unexpected as the melodies you've brought to our lives."

Morros, his guarded demeanor softened, gave a

small nod. "Farewell, Elania. May your journey be as exhilarating as our battles."

Elania turned her attention to Sylv, her heart a swirl of emotions. Their eyes met, a silent conversation passing between them. "Thank you, Sylv, for igniting a spark within me that I thought was lost."

Sylv's embrace was tender yet resolute. "You're a part of our story now, Elania. Don't forget that."

As the sun dipped below the horizon, bathing the land in hues of pink and gold, the Fortuitous Few and their new companions, Sylv and Kala, embarked on their journey to deliver the package to Jaral Haunthnor. The path stretched before them, a rugged tapestry woven with rocky hills and narrow trails that demanded unwavering focus. The ground, uneven and unforgiving, crunched beneath their boots, and the air held a faint hint of minerals and the promise of adventure.

Kala's presence was a pillar of strength, his form a reassuring silhouette against the changing sky. His warhammer, a testament to his resilience, rested on his shoulder. An unspoken unity flowed between him and the group, an understanding that they would face whatever challenges lay ahead together.

As they traversed the challenging terrain, their camaraderie found voice in shared stories and laughter, a harmonious melody that echoed against the stark surroundings. Rashe's lute added a layer of enchantment to their journey, each note a brushstroke painting the canvas of their memories.

Their laughter, however, was interrupted by a deep, rumbling tremor that seemed to arise from the very heart of the earth. The ground quaked beneath them, and a colossal figure emerged from the shadows, its stony visage an awe-inspiring sight against the landscape's raw beauty.

Adran's voice was filled with awe as he observed the stone guardian. "This is a sight to behold, a living embodiment of the land."

Sylv's grip on his weapon tightened, his eyes fixed on the approaching guardian. "Prepare yourselves! We're about to face an opponent unlike any before!"

The stone guardian, a towering marvel of stone and earth, moved with an uncanny grace that belied its colossal form. Its luminous eyes glinted with an almost sentient awareness as they settled on the group, and with a primal roar, it lunged forward, its massive fists cleaving through the air.

The ensuing battle was a symphony of clash and echo, the ring of metal against stone punctuated by grunts and calls of determination. Kala's warhammer swung with a thunderous force, each strike creating hairline fractures on the guardian's rugged surface. Adran's ethereal energy enveloped him, granting him an otherworldly agility as he engaged the creature in an intricate dance of offense and defense.

Bevin's staff spun like an extension of himself, creating a protective whirlwind that shielded his companions from the guardian's onslaught. Morros darted through the fray, his daggers glinting in the sunlight as he deftly exploited weaknesses in the guardian's defense.

Sylv's blade moved with a fluid grace, each stroke a testament to his mastery. He weaved through the battle like a dancer, his strikes precise and calculated. He deflected blows with expert parries, his focus unwavering amidst the chaos.

The battle raged on, the guardian's stony form showing signs of wear, cracks spiderwebbing across its exterior. The Fortuitous Few fought valiantly, each member of the group sustaining injuries as they pressed on, their determination unwavering.

With a final, thunderous blow from Kala's warhammer, the guardian's form shattered, a breathtaking cascade of rubble that danced like a waterfall frozen in time. The group stood panting, sweat-slicked and bruised, victorious.

As the dust began to settle, the treasure hidden within the guardian's heart was unveiled. Gleaming gems of every color and size spilled forth, their luminous facets casting prismatic glimmers in the fading light. Precious metals intertwined with the jewels, creating a breathtaking mosaic of wealth and wonder.

Morros' eyes widened, his voice a hushed whisper. "By all the realms, we've stumbled upon a king's ransom!"

Sylv's grin was a mixture of exhaustion and exhilaration, his gaze sweeping over the trove. "A formidable battle, and a reward that matches the challenge."

Kala's deep laughter resonated like a rumble of thunder. "Fortune favors those who dare to test their mettle."

With their wounds tended and the treasure securely stowed, the group continued their journey towards Jaral Haunthnor. The path remained as arduous as ever, the terrain unyielding, yet their spirits remained resolute.

As the sun sank below the horizon, painting the sky in vivid shades of orange and purple, they pressed forward, united in purpose. The memory of their hard-fought triumph and the bonds they had forged fueled their steps. The journey ahead was uncertain, but their camaraderie and shared determination made them unstoppable.

The future held untold adventures and challenges, yet the Fortuitous Few and their newfound companions, Sylv and Kala, ventured forth with heads held high. They were a tapestry of unique individuals, woven together by destiny's threads, ready to face whatever the world had in store for them. And as the stars began to twinkle in the emerging night sky, they embraced the unknown with open hearts, united in their unwavering pursuit of greatness.

With their steps carrying them deeper into the rugged landscape, the Fortuitous Few and their companions stumbled upon a small, hidden cave nestled within the rocky hills. The entrance was narrow, almost concealed by the jagged terrain, but it beckoned to them like a welcoming embrace. As they ventured inside, the air grew cool and damp, a stark contrast to the harshness of the outside world.

"Looks like we've found our shelter for the night," Bevin remarked, his staff illuminating the cave's interior.

Sylv nodded in agreement. "A fortunate discovery indeed. Let's set up camp here and take shifts for watch."

Their fatigue was palpable as they set about creating a makeshift campsite. A fire crackled in the center, its warm glow providing a sense of comfort amidst the cave's shadows. Bedrolls were spread out, and rations were shared among the weary travelers.

As night settled in, the group agreed to take shifts

to keep watch. Adran, ever vigilant, took the first watch. His keen senses were attuned to the subtlest shifts in the cave's atmosphere, and his elven eyes pierced the darkness. It was during his watch that he noticed a faint glimmer in the corner of the cave. Investigating further, he discovered a cluster of luminescent mushrooms, their soft glow casting an ethereal radiance over the cave's walls. He marveled at the beauty of this natural wonder, a moment of tranquility amidst the journey's chaos.

Rashe, who had been strumming his lute softly, took over the watch from Adran. The melodies he played seemed to harmonize with the gentle whispers of the cave, a serenade to the night itself. During his watch, Rashe's acute hearing caught the distant sound of rushing water. Curiosity piqued, he ventured deeper into the cave, his path illuminated by the luminescent mushrooms. To his surprise, he discovered a small underground stream, its clear waters glistening in the faint light. He knelt by the water's edge, allowing its soothing song to wash over him, a hidden oasis in the heart of the earth.

Morros' shift came next, his cat-like eyes scanning the cave's entrance for any signs of danger. His senses were finely tuned, and he detected the faint rustle of movement from the shadows. He approached cautiously, his fingers curling around the hilt of his dagger. To his relief, the source of the sound was a family of small creatures, their curious eyes reflecting the firelight. Morros observed them with a mixture of amusement and wonder, a reminder of the diverse inhabitants that shared their world.

Kala, his massive form huddled near the fire, took over the watch from Morros. His imposing presence seemed to fill the cave, and his eyes never wavered from the entrance. During his watch, Kala's sharp senses detected a faint scent on the breeze, carried by the draft that flowed through the cave. He followed the scent to a crevice in the wall, where he discovered a cluster of rare and fragrant herbs. He carefully plucked a few leaves, a potential boon for future journeys.

Bevin, his scholarly demeanor lending an air of tranquility, assumed the final watch. His gaze was fixed on the dancing flames, lost in thought. During his watch, a soft voice seemed to whisper to him, guiding his attention to a wall adorned with intricate carvings. He traced the patterns with his fingers, realizing that they depicted scenes from an ancient tale. It was a glimpse into the past, a connection to the history of the land they now traversed.

As the night gave way to the soft hues of dawn, the weary adventurers stirred from their slumber, each having experienced a unique connection to the cave's mysteries during their watch. The cave, once a hidden sanctuary, had become a tapestry of shared moments, a testament to the bond forged among them.

With their watches complete and a new day ahead, the Fortuitous Few and their companions emerged from the cave, their spirits renewed and hearts lightened by the treasures they had uncovered within its depths. The journey continued, each step carrying them closer to their destination and the unknown adventures that awaited them. As the sun painted the sky with hues of gold and amber, they walked forward with heads held high, united by the experiences they had shared and the unbreakable bond that had formed between them.

Chapter 20

As the sun painted the sky in shades of brilliance, the Fortuitous Few and their newfound companions resumed their journey, leaving behind the sheltering embrace of the cave. The air was crisp and invigorating, carrying with it a sense of renewed purpose. They walked with determination, the terrain gradually transitioning from the rocky hills to a more open expanse, dotted with patches of wildflowers and meandering streams.

Several hours into their trek, the distant sounds of struggle reached their ears, carried on the wind like a haunting melody. The group quickened their pace, their instincts on high alert. As they rounded a bend in the path, the scene that unfolded before them was one of chaos and desperation.

Four hulking orc bandits surrounded a terrified family—a human father, mother, a girl of fourteen, and a young boy of eight. The father's face was etched with pain, his body battered and bloodied from the relentless onslaught of the orcs. The mother held her children close, her eyes filled with a mixture of fear and fierce determination.

Without hesitation, Adran sprang into action. His ethereal energy enveloped him as he moved swiftly to the injured father's side. His hands glowed with a gentle light as he worked to stabilize the man's injuries, a calm and steady presence amidst the chaos.

Sylv, his expression a mask of unwavering resolve, drew his blade with a fluid motion. His voice carried across the battleground, firm and commanding. "Leave these innocents alone, or you'll face the consequences."

Rashe's fingers danced on the strings of his lute, the melody he played weaving through the air like a protective barrier. It was a tune of courage and defiance, a harmonious counterpoint to the orc's harsh growls.

Morros, a shadow among shadows, emerged from the periphery. His daggers gleamed with a deadly promise as he positioned himself strategically, ready to strike when the opportunity presented itself.

Kala's massive form loomed like a mountain, a silent guardian watching over the family. His warhammer rested in his grasp, its weight a testament to his strength and determination.

The orcs hesitated, eyeing the formidable group before them. A tense standoff ensued, the air thick with uncertainty. In a voice that carried both menace and desperation, the orc leader barked, "Stand aside, and we'll let the humans go."

Sylv's grip tightened on his blade. "Release them now, and you may leave with your lives."

The standoff continued, the balance of power hanging by a thread. But the orcs were not prepared for the unyielding resolve of the Fortuitous Few and their companions.

The clash erupted like a thunderous symphony of steel and magic, a crescendo of chaos and valor that reverberated through the air like a battle hymn. The orc leader's bellowing challenge hung like a dark omen, a chilling prelude to the impending clash that would decide the fate of this rugged terrain.

With a fierce battle cry, the orcs surged forward, their brutish forms emerging from the shadows like monstrous apparitions against the unforgiving landscape. Their war cries echoed like primal thunder, a proclamation of their intent to crush all opposition in their path.

Morros, a shadow in perpetual motion, blurred the lines between man and phantom as he darted between his adversaries with preternatural agility. His twin daggers became extensions of his very being, their lethal dance a symphony of deadly precision. Orcs stumbled and faltered, their roars of aggression turning into anguished cries as Morros struck with blinding speed, leaving behind a trail of crimson despair.

Adran's fists blazed with an otherworldly energy as he met the first orc head-on, a collision that sent shockwaves rippling through the battlefield. The ground quaked beneath their feet as the orc was hurled back, its body colliding with the earth in a violent symphony of impact. Adran's aura pulsed with ethereal light, an embodiment of his unwavering resolve to shield the innocent from the storm of violence.

Rashe's music swelled, a haunting melody that cut through the chaos like a clarion call. His lute, an instrument of both artistry and defiance, resonated with a pulse of energy that enshrouded his companions. The chords reverberated through the air like an invisible shield, woven from threads of courage and determination that fortified their spirits for the battle ahead.

Kala, a towering titan of raw power, swung his warhammer with bone-shattering force, the very air trembling with the might of his blows. Each strike was a seismic event, its echoes reverberating through the ground as orc defenses shattered like fragile glass. Orcs were sent sprawling, their twisted forms sprawled across the unforgiving terrain, victims of Kala's unrelenting might as he carved a path of devastation through their ranks.

Sylv's blade danced with deadly grace, an intricate tapestry of lethal elegance that wove through the chaos with fluid precision. He moved like a maestro orchestrating a symphony of death, his strikes a calculated masterpiece of blade and body. The orc leader, a hulking beast of fury, lunged with a ferocious roar, but Sylv's blade met the challenge with a resounding clash that sent sparks cascading through the air. The collision of steel against steel echoed through the very core of the battlefield, a reverberation of power and defiance that symbolized the clash of wills.

The battle raged on, a tempest of frenzied desperation as the orcs fought with savage intensity, their primal instincts driving them to lash out against their adversaries. But with every blow struck by the Fortuitous Few, the orcs' resistance wavered, their once-ferocious attacks diminishing into feeble, desperate attempts to cling to life.

One by one, the orcs fell, their bodies crumpling to the unforgiving ground like discarded marionettes. Morros's daggers danced with unerring accuracy, finding vital points with surgical precision. Adran's ethereal energy repelled their advances, his celestial might an impenetrable barrier against their savagery. Rashe's music, an anthem of valor, emboldened his allies and struck fear into the hearts of their enemies. Kala's warhammer shattered bone and armor alike, its brutal impact leaving nothing but devastation in its wake. And Sylv's blade, an extension of his unwavering determination, carved a path of triumph through the chaos, each stroke a testament to his skill and unwavering resolve.

The orc leader, a towering colossus of brutality, finally met his end in a climactic clash with Sylv. The clash of steel against steel resonated through the air like a thunderclap, a crescendo of power that climaxed in a final, definitive strike. Sylv's blade, an arc of death and destiny, found its mark with unerring accuracy, severing the leader's final thread of resistance and ending his reign of terror.

With the battle won, the Fortuitous Few stood amidst a scene of both victory and solemnity. The echoes of battle faded, replaced by the soft rustling of leaves and the distant songs of birds, as if nature itself bore witness to their valor.

Amidst the aftermath of the intense battle, the Fortuitous Few and their newfound companions turned their attention to the injured father. His face was etched with pain, and his body bore the marks of the brutal encounter with the orc bandits. Adran's healing touch had provided some measure of relief, but it was evident that the man needed further medical attention, and the journey to Cavranosk was far from easy.

Sylv's gaze held a steely determination as he spoke, his voice a reassuring anchor amidst the uncertainty that lingered in the air. "We'll accompany you to Cavranosk. Your family will receive the care they need."

Sylv's gaze flickered with concern as he looked around at his companions, his mind racing to find a solution. It was Bevin, the skilled survivalist of the group, who stepped forward with a determined expression. Bevin's agile fingers worked deftly as he assessed their surroundings and the materials available.

"Listen up," Bevin's voice was firm but reassuring, "we need to fashion a makeshift stretcher for the father. We'll need something sturdy to carry him on, and I've spotted a couple of large branches that could work as the frame."

Adran, his brow furrowed with concentration, nodded in agreement. "Indeed, that could work. We should also gather some strong vines or rope to secure the branches together."

Together, Bevin and Adran set to work. Bevin skillfully detached two long, sturdy branches from nearby trees, his fingers working with precision honed from years of surviving in the woods and resourcefulness. Adran, his ethereal energy still shimmering faintly, lent his strength to the task, helping to position the branches in a way that would provide stability and support.

As the makeshift frame took shape, Bevin's gaze swept the area, and he spotted a cluster of thick vines hanging from a nearby tree. With nimble fingers, he climbed the tree and skillfully detached the vines, lowering them to Adran below.

"These should do the trick," Bevin called down, a hint of triumph in his voice.

Adran nodded in approval as he worked alongside Bevin, using the vines to secure the branches together. The result was a rugged but sturdy stretcher, a testament to their ingenuity and teamwork.

"Good work, Bevin," Adran's voice held a note of gratitude as he stepped back to survey their creation. "Now, we'll need something soft to cushion the stretcher and make the journey more bearable for the father."

Rashe, always attuned to the world around him, had been collecting patches of moss and soft leaves. He stepped forward, a gentle smile on his lips, as he laid down the natural cushioning atop the stretcher.

"We can use these moss and leaves to create a relatively comfortable surface," Rashe explained, his voice a soothing melody in the midst of their preparations.

The injured father, his eyes half-lidded from pain, managed a weak smile of gratitude as he was carefully positioned onto the makeshift stretcher. The Fortuitous Few worked together, their movements synchronized and purposeful, as they secured the father onto the stretcher with care.

"Alright, we're ready to move," Bevin's voice held a note of determination as he gestured for Kala and Sylv to take hold of the stretcher's handles on either side.

The group moved as one, the stretcher held aloft with a newfound sense of purpose. Adran walked alongside, his healing energy a reassuring presence that radiated with warmth and comfort.

The journey ahead was arduous, the path fraught with uneven terrain and hidden challenges. But as the Fortuitous Few carried the injured father on their makeshift stretcher, their steps were imbued with a shared resolve to see their mission through. Bevin and Adran's ingenuity and resourcefulness had not only created a practical solution but had also strengthened the bonds of camaraderie that bound them together. As they moved forward, the sun casting its golden glow upon their path, they were a testament to the power of unity and compassion in the face of adversity.

While on their journey Rashe began to play

a joyous and healing tune on his ocarina. The
harmonious tune encircled the entire party and
their new companions healing them from some
of their wounds from the encounter with the orcs.
The tune was a familiar one to everyone and the
young daughter of the family began to sing the
accompanying lyrics as Rashe played.

In realms of magic and mystic light,
Where courage and honor take their flight,
A melody sweet, a healing song,
Shall rise from hearts, both brave and strong.
Hear the joyful song of healing, pure and bright,
Guiding souls from darkness into the light,
With every note, with every rhyme,
Hope and restoration for all time.

In dungeons deep and forests wide,
Where heroes stand with valor and pride,
A soothing tune, a balm so deep,
Shall mend the wounds and banish sleep.

Hear the joyful song of healing, pure and bright,
Guiding souls from darkness into the light,
With every note, with every rhyme,
Hope and restoration for all time.

Through battles fought with sword and spell,
The wounded find solace, make haste to dwell,

A chorus of hearts, united in grace,
Bringing comfort and warmth in this sacred space.

Hear the joyful song of healing, pure and bright,
Guiding souls from darkness into the light,
With every note, with every rhyme,
Hope and restoration for all time.

So let us sing, our voices strong,
A tapestry woven, a harmony long,
A tapestry woven, a harmony long...

Hear the joyful song of healing, pure and bright,
Guiding souls from darkness into the light,
With every note, with every rhyme,
Hope and restoration for all time.

In realms of magic and mystic light,
Where courage and honor take their flight,
This melody lives, forever shall ring,
A song of healing, with joy we sing.

Rashe approached the young girl with a warm smile, his eyes twinkling with genuine admiration. "My dear, your voice carries the grace of a woodland stream and the purity of a starlit night. Your talent is a rare and precious gift, a melody that touches the heart and soothes the soul."

The girl's eyes widened in surprise and delight,

her cheeks flushing with a mixture of shyness and happiness. She glanced at her family, who nodded in agreement and encouragement.

"Thank you," she murmured softly, her voice filled with a mixture of humility and newfound confidence. "I've always loved singing, but I never thought anyone would truly enjoy hearing me."

Rashe placed a hand on her shoulder, his touch gentle and reassuring. "Oh, but your voice has the power to uplift spirits and bring joy to those around you. It's a gift that should be cherished and shared."

The rest of the group nodded in agreement, their expressions reflecting the sincerity of Rashe's words. Adran added, "In the midst of our adventures, it's these moments of beauty and talent that remind us of the light that exists even in the darkest of times."

Sylv chimed in with a warm smile, "Your song, like a beacon of hope that brings warmth to our hearts. Remember, your voice is a treasure that can inspire and uplift all of those that are lucky enough to hear it."

The young girl's shyness seemed to melt away, replaced by a sense of newfound purpose. With a grateful nod, she replied, "I'll keep singing, then. Maybe I can bring a bit of light to others, just like your songs have done for us."

Rashe patted her shoulder gently and looked

around at the group, his eyes filled with pride. "Music, like camaraderie, has the power to mend wounds and strengthen bonds. Let us continue our journey, hearts uplifted by both song and friendship."

The Fortuitous Few and their companions pressed on along the winding path as they embarked on the next leg of their journey. The air seemed to carry a newfound sense of camaraderie, the bonds between the group and their rescued companions growing stronger with each step. The continuation of joyful song and music from Rashe, the bard, and his newly acclaimed troubadour was like a melody woven into the fabric of their shared adventure.

The young girl with a voice that held the purity of innocence and the promise of untamed potential, eagerly joined Rashe in another tune. Her voice harmonized with Rashe's melodies, creating an enchanting duet that resonated through the open landscape. The notes seemed to dance on the wind, lifting the spirits of all who heard them. The trilling of the troubadour's voice was like a soothing balm, mending the wounds of battle and enhancing the magic that poured from Rashe's ocarina. .

As the day wore on and the sun began its descent toward the horizon, the group's footsteps fell in time with the rhythm of the music. Soon the group could see Cavranosk just a short distance away. The mother of the children waved her hands up high towards the guards that stood outside the town to bring attention to them with hope they would come and relieve their weary new friends from carrying her husband. She could see that two guards recognized her and quickly made their way out to assist them on the final leg of the journey.

Chapter 21

Upon their arrival in the hamlet of Cavranosk, the healers wasted no time in attending to the injured father. His wounds, sustained during the harrowing encounter with the marauding orcs, had left him in a state of dire need. Beads of sweat glistened on their brows as they worked diligently to mend his battered form, their fingers guided by both skill and desperation.

Meanwhile, the leader of the village guard, a weathered figure with eyes that held the weight of countless struggles, approached the Fortuitous Few. Gratitude flowed from his every word as he extended a warm welcome, expressing his deep appreciation for the aid they had rendered to the family they had encountered on their journey. His voice, tinged with a sense of community and resilience, spoke volumes about the strength of this humble hamlet.

"We are but a meager settlement, our lives centered around the toil of wheat farming and the ceaseless turning of our mill," he explained with a gracious nod, acknowledging the modesty of their offering. "However, you are more than guests here; you are now part of our shared story. Tonight, as the sun dips beneath the horizon, you are invited to partake in our communal meal, a feast of simple yet hearty fare, and to join us in the age-old tradition of storytelling."

Rashe, ever the eloquent bard, offered a sincere nod of appreciation to the guard, his eyes reflecting both gratitude and curiosity. With their bodies aching from the long and arduous journey, the prospect of rest was an enticing one.

"Thank you for your warm welcome," Rashe replied, his voice holding the gentle lilt of a storyteller. "We have traveled far, and the weariness in our bones yearns for respite. Could you kindly direct us to a place where we might find rest after our arduous walk?"

With a hospitable gesture, the guard led them to a humble building nearby. It was a structure primarily used for housing migrant farm workers during the harvest season, yet it held a certain rustic charm. Several simple beds lined the room, offering a haven for the exhausted travelers. Adjacent to this shelter, a small shed concealed the village's privy and a modest bathhouse, promising a chance to wash away the dust of the road.

One by one, the weary members of the party took their turns in the bathhouse, each sigh of relief echoing the profound exhaustion they felt. While some sought solace in slumber, others reveled in the rejuvenating warmth of the bath. In this tranquil moment, they found themselves not only cleansed of the journey's grime but also embraced by the warm hospitality of Cavranosk, a village that had opened its heart to the Fortuitous Few in their time of need.

Amidst their well-earned rest and cleansing rituals, a young farmhand entered the room bearing a tray laden with provisions, an embodiment of the village's hospitality. On this humble platter lay a jug brimming with crisp, clear well water, a cask holding the warmth of locally-sourced wine, delicate goblets for sharing, and a platter adorned with freshly baked bread. This bread, kissed by golden hues and infused with fragrant herbs cultivated in the village, promised not just sustenance but a glimpse into the very essence of Cavranosk's culinary traditions.

The aromatic bouquet of freshly baked bread mingled gracefully with the fragrant herbs, evoking a symphony for the senses that sang of the land's abundance. Each slice of bread, with its crispy crust and tender interior, seemed to carry the artisanal touch of Cavranosk's bakers, a testament to their skill and the love infused into every loaf.

As the scene unfolded before them, Sylv, freshly invigorated from his bath, made his way back into the room. His eyes alighted upon the generous offerings, and a warm and appreciative smile graced his lips. Approaching the young farmhand, he extended his gratitude for the thoughtful refreshments.

"Your kindness is truly appreciated," Sylv remarked, his voice carrying the weight of gratitude and his eyes reflecting a genuine appreciation.

The young farmhand's response was punctuated by a heartfelt revelation, his eyes carrying the weight of familial ties. "He's my uncle, you know," he confided, his voice tinged with a mix of relief and affection. "Your aid in bringing him back means the world to my family. We feared we might lose him to the perils of that road."

Sylv nodded, his expression one of understanding and empathy. "Your uncle is a brave man, and he fought valiantly. Bringing your uncle home safely was a matter of honor and duty, but your generosity warms our hearts."

A warm and genuine smile spread across the young man's face. "It's no more than you deserve," he replied, his tone infused with the sincerity that seemed to permeate every corner of Cavranosk. "In our village, we believe in looking out for one another. You've become a part of our story, and we're proud to have you at our table."

With those words, the farmhand retreated with a polite nod, leaving Sylv and the others to savor the simple yet profound gesture of camaraderie. The bread's crust yielded to a soft and flavorful interior, and the wine, though humble in origin, bore the distinct taste of the land's labor. As they indulged in these offerings, it became evident that their journey had not only forged alliances but also illuminated the beauty of the shared human experience, where kindness and gratitude transcended words.

As Sylv and his companions broke bread together, the room was filled with the sounds of easy camaraderie and laughter. Each bite of the rustic fare seemed to strengthen not just their bodies but also the bonds that had formed among them. The wine, rich with the essence of the land, seemed to flow not only in their cups but also through the very spirit of the gathering, weaving a tapestry of goodwill and mutual respect. The air was thick with tales of past adventures and hopeful whispers of journeys yet to come, as each person shared a piece of their story, enriching the collective narrative of those present.

Outside, the evening sun dipped below the horizon, casting a golden hue over the village of Cavranosk. The warmth of the setting sun seemed to mirror the warmth within the room, a beacon of light in a world that often knew too much darkness. Sylv, looking out the window, felt a sense of peace settle over him. Here, in this small village, with these resilient and kind-hearted people, he found a sense of belonging that he had not known he was seeking. The challenges of the road ahead seemed less daunting, bolstered by the strength of newfound friendships and the enduring power of human kindness.

As the night deepened and the fire's glow dimmed to embers, Rashe quietly retrieved his old, well-loved lute. With a gentle touch, he began to strum a soft, melodic tune, its notes weaving through the room like a gentle breeze. The music, both haunting and soothing, seemed to capture the essence of their journey - the sorrows, the joys, and the unbreakable bond they shared. One by one, each member of the group found comfort in their chosen spots, closing their eyes to the lullaby that Rashe offered with every tender pluck of the strings.

The melody floated up to the rafters, mingling with the night sounds of the village and the distant murmur of the wind. Sylv, lying on a makeshift bed of straw and blankets, felt a profound sense of gratitude. The music was a reminder of the resilience of the mortal spirit and the ability to find beauty and hope even in the darkest of times. As he drifted off to sleep, the soft strumming of the lute anchoring him in a dreamlike state, he felt more than ever connected to his companions, to the village, and to the winding road that lay ahead. The night embraced them all, cradled in the harmony of Rashe's lullaby, promising another day of adventure with the rise of the sun.

The following morning dawned bright and clear, casting a golden light over the village of Cavranosk. The air was filled with the fresh scents of morning dew and newly baked bread. The Fortuitous Few awoke, rejuvenated by a night of peaceful rest, greeted by the friendly faces of the villagers who had already started their day. Breakfast was a communal affair, with everyone gathered around a large wooden table laden with simple yet hearty fare. The laughter and chatter of the villagers mingled with the chirping of birds, creating a symphony of rural life.

As the day unfolded, the party decided to lend their hands to the villagers, an expression of gratitude for the hospitality they had received. They split up, each joining different groups of locals in their daily tasks. Sylv found himself assisting in the fields, tilling the land alongside the farmers, his arms growing accustomed to the rhythm of the work. Rashe, with his gentle demeanor and quick fingers, helped the village seamstress repair and sew garments, while others in their group tended to the maintenance of buildings and pathways. The day passed in a blur of activity, laughter, and shared stories, as the villagers and the travelers found common ground in their toil and aspirations.

As evening approached, the group regathered, each with new friends and tales of their day's adventures. They shared a meal with the villagers, this time contributing to the preparation and cooking. The food tasted better with the added ingredient of their own labor and the joy of shared experiences. The evening was spent in merriment, with music, dancing, and the exchange of stories under the stars. The bonds forged with the people of Cavranosk were not just of gratitude but of a deeper connection, one that transcended the briefness of their stay. Sylv and his companions went to bed that night, hearts full of the day's memories, knowing that they had not only received kindness but had also given something precious back to this charming village.

Chapter 22

The undulating hills of Lacronshire stood as sentinels over the hamlet of Cavranosk, their rugged contours softened by the evening sun that bathed the sky in molten hues of orange and purple. Below, nestled amidst fields and woodlands, the hamlet lay quiet, unaware of the malevolent gaze fixed upon it from the shadowed thickets above.

Hidden among the ancient trees, their gnarled branches twisted like skeletal fingers, a party of orc raiders gathered. They were a grim sight, their hulking forms cloaked in crude armor that bore the scars of countless battles. The fading sunlight cast long shadows across their grotesque faces, their sharp teeth glinting as they exchanged sinister grins. The fading light seemed to mimic the doom they intended to unleash, snuffing out hope as nightfall crept closer.

The orcs spoke in hushed tones, their guttural voices a dissonant melody of malice. "The granaries are full," one of them snarled, his bloodshot eyes glinting with greed. "Gold in their coffers, and plenty of livestock. We'll feast like kings."

Another, taller and more menacing, spat on the ground and grinned. "Not just livestock. The villagers will learn to serve us, or they'll die screaming."

A cruel laugh rippled through the group as they reveled in their vile fantasies. The innocent laughter and faint melodies drifting up from Cavranosk only stoked their twisted desires. In their minds, the men were but feeble obstacles, and the women and children mere chattel to be enslaved. Their hearts, if they could be called that, were as black as the shadows thickening around them.

Yet, as the cold wind swept through the forest, rustling leaves and bending grass, it seemed to carry a warning, a low, mournful sound that made even the raiders pause. The gnarled branches above them swayed as if whispering secrets to the gathering night.

But the orcs, drunk on their own malice, dismissed the foreboding air. They failed to notice the resilience etched into the land below—the way Cavranosk's fields bore the weight of generations, the quiet strength in the sturdy stone walls of the hamlet, and most importantly, the guardians who had already pledged their lives to defend it.

As the sun sank lower, casting Cavranosk in a

muted golden glow, the village's atmosphere grew tense. Makeshift barricades lined the streets, hastily constructed from overturned carts, barrels, and timber. Villagers huddled behind these defenses, their faces a canvas of fear and grim determination. Farmers gripped pitchforks and scythes, their knuckles white, while others carried hunting bows or ancient swords handed down through generations. The laughter of children had been replaced by the heavy silence of anticipation.

Inside the village square, Sylv stood before the assembled defenders. His armor gleamed faintly in the dying light, and his sword rested casually against his shoulder, though his expression was anything but casual. His voice carried over the murmuring crowd, calm yet commanding. "We stand united, not as strangers, but as protectors of this village. These orcs seek to destroy what we hold dear, to defile what we've built. Tonight, we show them that we will not falter. We fight, not for glory, but for each other."

The villagers raised their voices in a ragged but defiant cheer. Among them were Morros, his twin daggers glinting as he crouched in the shadows, ever the silent predator; Bevin, his sharp eyes scanning the treetops as he nocked an arrow; Kala, a veritable mountain of muscle, his warhammer resting easily in his massive hands; Adran, a beacon of calm amidst the storm, his celestial aura emanating a quiet reassurance; and Rashe, clutching his ocarina, a determined look on his face as he prepared to transform fear into resolve with his melodies.

The first sound of the attack came like a drumbeat of doom—low, rhythmic thuds reverberating through the forest. The orcish war drums grew louder, an unholy symphony that seemed to vibrate in the marrow of those who heard it. The defenders exchanged nervous glances, the oppressive sound seeping into their bones.

Then, the forest erupted. The orcs emerged from the shadows, their grotesque forms silhouetted against the twilight. Their leader, a monstrous brute with a twisted grin and a jagged axe that seemed to drip malice, raised his weapon and let out a guttural roar. The sound echoed across the battlefield, a chilling overture to the carnage to come.

"Hold your ground!" Sylv shouted, his voice cutting through the chaos like a blade.

The defenders answered with a volley of arrows. Bevin's shots were precise, striking down orcs before they could reach the barricades, while others fired with trembling hands. The orcs, undeterred, surged forward, their brutish strength shattering obstacles in their path.

Morros was a blur of motion, his daggers slicing through the chaos with deadly precision. He moved like a shadow, striking before his enemies even knew he was there. Each slash of his blades was lethal, leaving a trail of fallen foes in his wake.

Kala was a juggernaut, his warhammer swinging with bone-shattering force. The ground trembled beneath his blows, and orcs were sent flying, their twisted forms crumpling like broken dolls. His booming voice carried across the battlefield, a rallying cry that lifted the spirits of those around him.

Rashe's ocarina sang a melody of defiance, its haunting notes weaving a protective aura that seemed to shield the defenders from despair. His music carried through the night, bolstering courage and turning fear into determination.

Adran moved among the wounded, his hands glowing with celestial energy. He closed wounds, mended broken bones, and whispered words of encouragement to those on the brink of collapse. Each touch was a reminder that hope still burned, even in the darkest moments.

Bevin perched atop a cart, his bowstring singing as he loosed arrow after arrow. Each shaft found its mark, thinning the orcish ranks with unerring precision. His sharp eyes darted across the battlefield, ever vigilant for threats.

In the center of the chaos, Sylv faced the orc chieftain. The brute's axe swung in wide arcs, each strike sending sparks flying as Sylv deflected the blows with his sword. Their duel was a clash of titans, a deadly dance that shook the earth beneath their feet. The chieftain's guttural laughter only fueled Sylv's resolve.

"You think you can stop us, human?" the orc sneered, his voice dripping with disdain.

Sylv's blade flashed in the dim light, scoring a deep gash across the orc's side. "I don't think. I know."

The chieftain roared in pain and fury, redoubling his assault. Their blades clashed again and again, steel ringing against steel in a brutal symphony.

The defenders' line faltered under the relentless onslaught, but Sylv's voice rang out once more. "Hold the line! Fight for your families, for your homes!"

Rashe's music swelled, a crescendo that seemed to lift every defender's heart. Adran called upon the heavens, sending a radiant burst of light that blinded the orcs and gave the villagers a moment to regroup. Kala roared and charged, his hammer smashing through the enemy's ranks with renewed vigor.

At last, the chieftain faltered, his strength waning. Sylv seized the moment, driving his sword through the orc's chest. The brute let out a final, guttural roar before collapsing, his massive form crashing to the ground.

Leaderless and demoralized, the remaining orcs began to retreat. The defenders pressed forward, driving them back into the forest until the drums of doom faded into silence.

As the night gave way to dawn, the battlefield lay quiet. The defenders, though bloodied and battered, stood victorious. Cavranosk had survived. In the light of the rising sun, the hamlet's resilience shone brighter than ever—a testament to the courage of its people and the guardians who had fought to protect them.

Chapter 23

The battle raged on under the pale light of the moon, a tempest of blood and steel. Sylv could feel the weight of every blow exchanged with the orc chieftain, each strike a test of his endurance and skill. The brute was a juggernaut of muscle and fury, his every movement fueled by a savage desire to dominate. Around them, the defenders of Cavranosk fought valiantly, their courage a flickering flame against the overwhelming tide of darkness.

The clash of weapons and the guttural cries of orcs filled the air, mingling with the shouts of the villagers as they desperately held their line. Despite their resolve, the orcs' sheer numbers pressed them back step by step. Sylv caught glimpses of his companions amidst the chaos—Kala's massive warhammer swinging in deadly arcs, Bevin's arrows striking true from his perch atop a collapsed cart, and Morros darting through the shadows like a wraith, his daggers glinting in the moonlight. Each of them fought with unyielding determination, yet even they could not be everywhere at once.

Sylv dodged a sweeping blow from the chieftain's axe, the weapon carving a deep gouge into the earth where he had stood moments before. Sweat dripped into his eyes as he countered with a quick slash, his blade glancing off the orc's thick hide. The chieftain roared, his voice a primal sound that sent shivers down Sylv's spine. This was no ordinary foe—he was a leader, a force of nature, and Sylv knew that the battle's outcome rested on their duel.

On the other side of the battlefield, Rashe stumbled, his ocarina slipping from his fingers as an orc lunged toward him. He barely avoided the creature's blade, rolling to the side and scrambling to his feet. His heart pounded in his chest, but a glimmer of resolve ignited within him. He grabbed the ocarina and lifted it to his lips, his trembling fingers finding their place on the instrument.

The melody that emerged was unlike any he had played before. The haunting notes seemed to pierce through the cacophony of battle, reaching the ears of friend and foe alike. It was a song of defiance, its mournful tones laced with a fierce determination. The villagers, their spirits flagging under the weight of the onslaught, felt the music stir something deep within them. They tightened their grips on their weapons, their fear melting away as they stood shoulder to shoulder.

"Hold the line!" one of the villagers cried, his voice rising above the din. Inspired by Rashe's melody, they fought back with renewed vigor. Pitchforks and scythes clashed against crude orcish weapons, their wielders no longer cowed by the ferocity of their foes.

Amidst the chaos, Adran knelt beside a young villager who had been struck down, his lifeblood pooling in the dirt. The healer's hands glowed with an ethereal light as he worked, his voice steady despite the pandemonium around him. "Stay with me," he murmured, his words both a command and a prayer. The boy's wounds began to close, the divine energy knitting flesh and bone back together.

"You'll fight again," Adran said, meeting the boy's frightened gaze. "We need every soul who can stand."

The boy nodded weakly, and with Adran's help, he struggled to his feet. The healer turned his attention to another wounded defender, his hands never idle as he moved through the battlefield. Each life he saved was another thread in the fabric of their resistance, and he fought with the knowledge that every second mattered.

Bevin, perched atop his vantage point, loosed

arrow after arrow, each shot finding its mark with unerring precision. His keen eyes scanned the battlefield, seeking the greatest threats to their line. He saw Kala, surrounded by a knot of orcs, his warhammer a whirlwind of destruction. The giant warrior let out a bellowing roar as he swung, sending two foes flying and scattering the others.

"Kala, left!" Bevin shouted, drawing and firing in one smooth motion. His arrow struck an orc sneaking up behind the warrior, dropping it mid-charge. Kala shot him a quick nod of thanks before resuming his rampage.

Nearby, Morros slipped through the melee like a shadow, his twin daggers flashing in the dim light. He struck with precision, severing tendons and arteries before vanishing into the fray. His movements were almost hypnotic, a deadly dance that left a trail of fallen enemies in his wake.

But even as the defenders rallied, the orcs pressed on, their relentless assault threatening to over-whelm them. Sylv, locked in his deadly duel with the chieftain, knew they needed something more to turn the tide. Gritting his teeth, he parried a vicious blow and drove his blade into the orc's side. The chieftain howled in pain but fought on, his eyes blazing with fury.

Just as the defenders' strength began to falter, a brilliant flare of light erupted at the edge of the battlefield. All eyes turned toward the tree line, where a figure emerged, clad in robes that shimmered like starlight. It was the elder of Cavranosk, a man rarely seen outside the village shrine. In his hands, he carried a staff crowned with a glowing crystal that pulsed with an otherworldly energy.

The elder raised his staff, and the crystal blazed with an incandescent light that banished the shadows. A pulse of energy rippled outward, sweeping across the battlefield. The orcs recoiled, howling in anguish as the light seared their dark souls. Many turned and fled, their ferocity broken by the radiant force. Those who remained were visibly weakened, their movements sluggish and their eyes filled with fear.

"Stand together!" the elder cried, his voice strong despite his frail appearance. "The light of unity shall not falter!"

Seizing the moment, Sylv pressed his advantage against the chieftain. With a final, desperate strike, he plunged his blade into the orc's chest. The chieftain let out a guttural roar before collapsing, his massive form crumpling to the ground. A hush fell over the battlefield as the remaining orcs, leaderless and broken, fled into the night.

The defenders stood in stunned silence, the weight of their victory slowly sinking in. The battlefield was littered with the fallen, both friend and foe, and the air was heavy with the scent of blood and smoke. Slowly, the villagers began to cheer, their voices rising in a chorus of triumph and relief.

Exhausted yet triumphant, the Fortuitous Few began the grim task of tending to the wounded and honoring the dead. Adran moved through the crowd, his hands still glowing as he offered comfort and healing to those in need. Kala and Morros helped the villagers gather their fallen, their faces solemn as they worked. Bevin retrieved his arrows, his sharp eyes scanning the horizon for any sign of a counterattack.

Sylv stood at the edge of the battlefield, his sword still in hand, as he watched the first light of dawn break over the hills of Lacronshire. The village, though scarred by the night's events, stood resilient, a testament to the strength of its people and the courage of those who had come to its aid.

Rashe joined him, his ocarina hanging loosely in his hand. "We survived," the bard said quietly, his voice heavy with exhaustion.

"For now," Sylv replied, his tone somber. "But this is just one battle. The road ahead will be no less perilous."

Rashe nodded, his gaze distant. "Then we'll face it together, as we always have."

The two stood in silence, the promise of new

challenges looming on the horizon. But for this moment, at least, they could take solace in the knowledge that their unity had prevailed against the darkness. Together, they turned back toward the village, ready to face whatever came next.

Chapter 24

The days following the battle were a blur of activity. The hamlet of Cavranosk, though victorious, lay in ruins—a stark reminder of the cost of survival. Smoke still curled from the charred remains of homes, and the fields, once lush with crops, were now a patchwork of trampled earth and ash. Yet amidst the devastation, there was a glimmer of hope, a determination in the eyes of the villagers that had not been there before.

The Fortuitous Few, weary but resolute, knew their work was far from over. Cavranosk needed more than healing; it needed a foundation for the future, one built on strength, resilience, and unity.

Sylv stood in the town square, addressing the villagers who had gathered. Their faces bore the marks of sleepless nights and lingering fear, but also a flicker of hope. The elder, his radiant staff dimmed but still glowing faintly, stood by Sylv's side as a symbol of the village's spirit.

"You've proven your courage in the face of overwhelming odds," Sylv began, his voice firm and commanding. "But courage alone will not keep you safe. If Cavranosk is to endure, you must rebuild—not only your homes but also your strength. We will stand with you, for a time, to teach you how to defend what is yours."

The villagers murmured among themselves, uncertainty mingling with hope. The elder stepped forward, his presence quiet yet authoritative. "Your guidance will be a blessing, Sylv. We accept your offer, not as charity, but as a lesson we will carry forward. Cavranosk must rise stronger, for the sake of our children and their children."

With a collective nod, the villagers agreed. The first steps toward rebuilding their lives began.

Kala, with his immense strength and practical know-how, took charge of rebuilding the hamlet's physical structures. He led teams of villagers to clear rubble and salvage what could be reused. His booming voice carried across the worksite, offering instructions and encouragement.

"Reinforce those beams," he called to a group lifting a roof frame. "A strong foundation is the backbone of a home—and a village."

The villagers marveled at Kala's ability to lift heavy timbers single-handedly, but he made sure to guide them patiently, teaching techniques they could use long after he was gone. Under his direction, new homes began to rise, sturdier than before, their walls reinforced with stone and wood from the surrounding forests.

Meanwhile, Sylv focused on fortifying the hamlet's defenses. He walked the perimeter of the village, gesturing to strategic points where watchtowers could be built and barriers erected. "Every village needs eyes," he explained, pointing to the nearby hills. "The high ground will warn you of danger long before it arrives."

Working alongside the villagers, Sylv helped construct wooden palisades and train a small group to maintain a constant watch. He stressed the importance of vigilance, knowing that the safety of Cavranosk depended on it.

Adran dedicated himself to the wounded, his hands glowing with celestial light as he tended to their injuries. The healer worked tirelessly, his calm demeanor bringing solace to those in pain. He also took on apprentices, teaching them basic medical skills using herbs gathered from the surrounding forests.

"Healing is not just a gift," Adran told a young woman who had shown promise. "It is a responsibility. You must learn to care for your people, to be the light in their darkest hours."

The villagers watched in awe as Adran's magic mended broken bones and closed wounds, but it was his kindness and patience that left the deepest impression. Under his guidance, a small team of healers began to emerge, ready to carry on his work.

Bevin, the master archer, took charge of teaching the villagers how to wield bows. At the edge of a field, he set up targets and demonstrated the basics of archery. The villagers, many of whom had never held a weapon before, struggled at first, but Bevin's steady encouragement kept them going.

"Archery isn't about strength," he said, correcting a young man's stance. "It's about patience and focus. Trust in yourself, and the bow will do the rest."

Over time, the villagers grew more confident, their arrows finding their marks with increasing accuracy. Bevin made sure to praise their progress, fostering a sense of pride and accomplishment.

Morros, ever the shadowy figure, surprised everyone by taking on a small group to teach stealth and guerrilla tactics. "Not every fight is won face-to-face," he explained, his voice low but firm. "Sometimes, the shadows are your greatest ally."

His methods were unconventional, but effective. He led his trainees through the forest, teaching them to move silently, blend with their surroundings, and strike from the shadows. By the end of the week, the villagers had a small but capable group of scouts and skirmishers.

Even Rashe found his role in the village's transformation. Between lessons and labor, he played his ocarina, its uplifting melodies keeping spirits high. The villagers would often pause in their work to listen, their weariness forgotten as the music filled the air.

Rashe also composed ballads of the battle, immortalizing the courage and unity of the villagers. He performed these songs in the evenings, drawing laughter and tears in equal measure. His music became a symbol of hope, reminding everyone of what they had endured and what they could achieve together.

By the end of a fortnight, Cavranosk had been transformed. Wooden palisades encircled the hamlet, watchtowers stood vigilant against the horizon, and the villagers—once meek farmers—now carried weapons with a sense of purpose. Though still untested, they stood straighter, their fear tempered by newfound confidence.

The fields, too, began to recover. Under Kala's guidance, the villagers worked tirelessly to restore their crops, replanting seeds and clearing debris. The promise of a bountiful harvest glimmered in the distance, a testament to their resilience.

On the final evening of the Fortuitous Few's stay, the villagers held a feast to honor their protectors. Long tables were laden with roasted meats, fresh bread, and bowls of steaming stew. The air was filled with laughter and music as the villagers celebrated not only their survival but also their transformation.

Sylv stood to address the crowd, his voice carrying over the festivities. "You've proven yourselves stronger than you knew," he said, his tone firm but warm. "The road ahead will not be easy, but you are no longer helpless. You are defenders, protectors of your home. Never forget that strength comes not from a blade, but from unity."

The villagers erupted into cheers, lifting their mugs in a toast. The Fortuitous Few exchanged glances, their bond strengthened by the gratitude and determination they saw in these people. Each of them knew that their time in Cavranosk had been more than just a duty—it had been a reminder of why they fought, and what they stood for.

As the night stretched on, filled with joy and camaraderie, the hamlet of Cavranosk bid farewell to their protectors. The villagers, now stronger and more united than ever, looked toward the future with hope. And as the first light of dawn broke over the horizon, the Fortuitous Few prepared to take their leave, their hearts heavy with the bonds they had forged, but resolute in their purpose.

For though their time in Cavranosk had come to an end, their journey was far from over. Together, they would face whatever challenges lay ahead, carrying with them the lessons of courage, unity, and resilience they had shared with the people of this humble yet extraordinary hamlet.

Chapter 25

The morning dawned crisp and clear, the air alive with the scent of fresh earth and the hum of renewal. The village of Cavranosk, now fortified and resolute, stood in stark contrast to the battered hamlet the Fortuitous Few had first encountered. The companions gathered their belongings as villagers lined the square, their faces filled with a mixture of gratitude and hope. The bonds forged in blood and toil made this departure more than a farewell—it was a promise to protect and to remember.

The elder approached, his staff gleaming faintly in the morning light. His face bore the lines of wisdom and worry, a man burdened by the knowledge he was about to share. "Before you leave, there is something you should know," he said, his voice grave. "The orcs' attack was not a mere coincidence. They were drawn here by an artifact hidden in the hills to the north—a grimoire of great power, left behind by the Ancients."

The companions exchanged wary glances. Sylv, ever the pragmatist, stepped forward. "What kind of power are we talking about?"

The elder's expression darkened. "The grimoire holds the secrets of binding and unbinding life itself. Legends say it can restore strength to the weary, heal the broken, and even call forth forces long forgotten. But such power is dangerous. If it falls into the wrong hands, it could spell doom not only for Cavranosk but for the entire realm."

Sylv's jaw tightened as he absorbed the implications. "Then we cannot leave it here unguarded," he said firmly. "If we retrieve it, we can ensure its safety—and perhaps use its knowledge to strengthen your defenses."

The elder nodded and handed Sylv a map, its edges worn and its ink faded with age. "The path will not be easy," he warned. "The grimoire is guarded by ancient wards, and those who have sought it before have never returned."

"Sounds like our kind of adventure," Rashe said with a wry grin, slinging his lute over his shoulder. The tension in the group eased momentarily, the bard's humor a welcome reprieve.

As they departed, the villagers lined the path, their eyes filled with a mix of sadness and hope. Final words of gratitude and encouragement echoed as the group made their way toward the hills. A young farmhand, whose uncle the Fortuitous Few had saved, approached Sylv and pressed a small charm into his hand. "For luck," he said simply, his voice thick with emotion.

Sylv looked down at the charm—a crude carving of a sunburst, a symbol of light in the face of darkness. He nodded solemnly. "Thank you," he said, tucking it into his pouch.

The companions set off, their footsteps echoing against the cobbled path as the village faded into the distance. The hills of Lacronshire rose before them, bathed in the golden light of morning. The air carried a cool breeze, but an undercurrent of unease rippled through the landscape. Despite the challenges ahead, the Fortuitous Few felt a renewed sense of purpose.

The path to the grimoire's resting place grew more treacherous as they ventured deeper into the hills. At first, the terrain was mild, the grassy slopes dotted with wildflowers swaying gently in the breeze. But as the day wore on, the landscape shifted. The vibrant greens gave way to jagged rocks and sparse vegetation. The air grew colder, and the shadows cast by the looming cliffs seemed to lengthen unnaturally.

"Something's watching us," Bevin said quietly, his keen eyes scanning the ridges above. His hand hovered near the quiver at his back, ready to draw an arrow at the slightest provocation.

Sylv nodded, his grip tightening on the hilt of his sword. "Stay sharp. If the grimoire is as powerful as the elder claims, we won't be the only ones seeking it."

The group pressed on, their camaraderie bolstering their spirits even as the path grew more treacherous. Strange noises drifted through the air—distant howls, rustling in the underbrush, and whispers that seemed to come from nowhere. The companions remained vigilant, their weapons at the ready.

As the sun dipped below the horizon, they reached a narrow gorge that cut through the hills. The map marked this as the first significant landmark on their journey. Tall, ancient stones flanked the entrance, their surfaces etched with runes that glowed faintly in the twilight.

"These must be part of the wards the elder mentioned," Adran said, studying the runes closely. The celestial energy in his hands pulsed faintly, reacting to the ancient magic. "The runes are a warning… and a barrier. Only those deemed worthy can pass."

"What does that mean?" Kala asked, hefting his warhammer. "Worthy by whose standards?"

Before Adran could respond, the runes flared brightly, and a low rumble filled the air. The ground beneath their feet shook, and a figure emerged from the stones—a towering guardian made of earth and stone. Its eyes glowed with an intense golden light as it raised a massive arm, blocking their path.

"Here we go," Sylv muttered, drawing his blade. "We don't back down now."

The guardian moved with surprising speed for its size, its heavy fists crashing into the ground as the group scattered. Kala roared and charged, his warhammer striking the creature's arm with a thunderous crack. The blow left a dent, but the guardian retaliated swiftly, forcing him to leap back.

"Focus on its core!" Adran shouted, pointing to the glowing runes on the guardian's chest. "That's where the magic is concentrated!"

Bevin climbed a nearby boulder, his bow drawn. He loosed an arrow that struck the core, causing the guardian to stagger. "It's working! Keep it up!" he called.

Rashe began to play a quick, energizing tune on his ocarina, the notes weaving through the air and bolstering the group's movements. Morros darted in and out of the guardian's reach, his daggers carving into its joints to slow its movements.

The battle was intense, but their teamwork proved stronger. With one final, coordinated strike, Kala's hammer and Sylv's blade shattered the core. The guardian crumbled into rubble, its magic dissipating into the night.

Beyond the gorge, the path narrowed, twisting through a dense forest where the trees grew unnaturally close together. Their gnarled branches intertwined overhead, blocking out the moonlight and plunging the group into darkness. The air was thick with a strange, oppressive energy that made it hard to breathe.

As they moved deeper into the forest, whispers began to fill the air. At first, they were faint, like the rustling of leaves, but they grew louder and more distinct with each step. Voices called out to them, some pleading, others mocking.

"Turn back," a woman's voice whispered in Sylv's ear. He froze, his hand instinctively going to his sword. The voice was familiar—hauntingly so. It sounded like his mother, long dead.

"You're not real," he said firmly, shaking his head. "You can't trick me."

But the whispers persisted, targeting each of them in turn. Rashe faltered as a voice whispered of his failures. Kala clenched his fists as a mocking laugh echoed through the forest. Even Morros, usually unshaken, paused as a voice from his past whispered a secret he thought buried forever.

"It's the wards," Adran said, his voice steady despite the whispers. "They're testing us. Do not give in."

Together, they pressed on, resisting the voices that sought to unnerve them. The forest seemed endless, its twisting paths designed to disorient, but their determination held firm. When they finally emerged, the oppressive energy lifted, and they found themselves at the base of a steep hill.

The final leg of their journey brought them to the entrance of an ancient cavern. Its mouth was framed by stone pillars etched with glowing runes, similar to those at the gorge. The air here was heavy with power, a tangible force that seemed to hum just beneath the surface.

"This is it," Sylv said, his voice quiet but resolute. "Whatever lies ahead, we face it together."

The companions exchanged nods, their bond unspoken but unbreakable. They stepped into the cavern, the light of day fading behind them as the darkness enveloped them. The promise of the grimoire's power loomed before them, its secrets a beacon in the shadows, calling them forward into the unknown.

Chapter 26

T he air within the cavern was thick and still, carrying a faint metallic tang that set their nerves on edge. The dim glow of the runes lining the entrance provided just enough light to cast long shadows on the jagged walls, making every step feel like an intrusion into something ancient and sacred. The Fortuitous Few advanced cautiously, their weapons drawn and senses heightened.

"Stay close," Sylv instructed, his voice low but commanding. "We don't know what we're walking into."

Rashe's hand lingered on his lute, his other gripping the hilt of his short sword. Kala walked ahead, his warhammer resting on his shoulder, while Bevin kept an arrow nocked, scanning the darkness for movement. Morros slunk along the edges of the group, his steps silent as a shadow. Adran brought up the rear, his celestial magic casting a faint glow that painted the cavern walls with a soft, warm light.

As they delved deeper, the runes on the walls began to pulse, growing brighter with each step. The air grew colder, and a low hum began to vibrate through the stone. It was a sound that seemed to resonate in their bones, unsettling and otherworldly.

"This place feels alive," Adran murmured, his voice tinged with unease. "The wards are strong here, and they're watching us."

"Let them watch," Kala grunted. "If they try anything, they'll meet my hammer."

The tunnel opened into a vast chamber, the ceiling lost in darkness above. In the center of the room stood a massive stone pedestal, its surface engraved with glowing symbols. Surrounding it were six statues, each depicting a different warrior, their faces obscured by helmets and their weapons raised in eternal vigilance.

Sylv stepped forward, his eyes scanning the room for traps. "Be careful," he warned. "This feels like a test."

As if in response to his words, the statues began to move. Stone cracked and groaned as the figures came to life, their once-fixed weapons now swinging with lethal intent. Without hesitation, the statues charged, their footsteps shaking the ground.

"Formation!" Sylv barked, raising his sword to parry the first blow.

Kala met one of the statues head-on, his hammer colliding with its stone blade in a clash that echoed through the chamber. "They hit harder than they look!" he called out, dodging a follow-up strike.

Bevin loosed an arrow, the projectile embedding itself in a crack between the statue's stone plates. It staggered, but only briefly. "Aim for the joints!" he shouted, firing again.

Morros darted between the statues, his daggers finding weak points with precision. "They're slow," he observed, "but they don't tire."

Meanwhile, Rashe's ocarina rang out with a sharp, rallying tune, bolstering the group's movements. The music filled the chamber, cutting through the oppressive hum of the wards.

Adran stayed near the center, casting protective wards and healing injuries as they occurred. A wave of his hand closed a gash on Sylv's arm, while another sent a burst of divine energy to repel an advancing statue.

As the battle raged on, one of the statues turned its attention to Rashe. The bard, focused on maintaining his music, didn't notice the stone warrior advancing on him until it was too late. The statue's sword swung in a deadly arc, striking Rashe squarely in the chest and sending him flying across the chamber.

"Rashe!" Adran cried, rushing to his fallen companion.

The bard lay crumpled on the ground, his ocarina shattered beside him. Blood seeped from a deep wound in his chest, staining his tunic. His breaths were shallow, and his eyes fluttered as he struggled to stay conscious.

Sylv roared in fury, charging the statue that had struck Rashe. His blade danced with precision, chipping away at the stone until the warrior collapsed into rubble. "Adran, help him!" he shouted, his voice filled with desperation.

Adran knelt beside Rashe, his hands glowing with celestial energy. He pressed them to the bard's chest, channeling his magic into the wound. "Stay with me," he whispered, his voice trembling. "You're not leaving us."

The glow of Adran's magic began to fade, and a look of panic crossed his face. "The wound is too deep," he said, his voice breaking. "I…I can't heal it."

"No," Kala growled, standing guard over them as another statue approached. "You don't get to give up. Use whatever magic you have left!"

Adran shook his head, tears welling in his eyes. "It's not enough."

Sylv turned, his face pale but determined. "Adran, is there anything—anything—that can bring him back?"

Adran hesitated, then nodded slowly. "There's a spell…a resurrection. But it's dangerous. It requires immense energy, and it doesn't always work. The soul has to be willing to return."

"Do it," Sylv said without hesitation. "We can't lose him."

Adran nodded, his face set with grim determination. He placed both hands over Rashe's heart, his magic flaring brighter than ever before. A golden aura enveloped the bard's body as Adran began to chant, his voice resonating with celestial power. The air grew heavy, and the hum of the wards seemed to quiet, as if the cavern itself was holding its breath.

The spell took its toll on Adran. Beads of sweat formed on his brow, and his hands trembled as he poured every ounce of his energy into the incantation. The golden light pulsed, growing brighter and brighter until it was almost blinding.

"Come back to us, Rashe," Adran whispered, his voice barely audible over the magic's hum. "We need you."

For a moment, there was silence. Then, with a gasp, Rashe's chest rose, and his eyes flew open. He coughed weakly, his hand reaching for the shattered pieces of his ocarina.

"You…can't get rid of me that easily," he rasped, a faint smile tugging at his lips.

Relief washed over the group like a wave. Kala let out a booming laugh, slapping Sylv on the back. "He's tougher than he looks!"

Bevin lowered his bow, his shoulders relaxing for the first time since the battle began. "Glad to have you back, bard."

Adran collapsed to the ground, his energy completely spent. Sylv caught him before he could fall further, helping him sit upright. "You did it," Sylv said, his voice filled with gratitude. "You saved him."

Adran nodded weakly. "Let's just hope it was worth the cost."

With the statues defeated and Rashe stabilized, the group pressed on. The pedestal in the center of the chamber had begun to glow, its runes shifting to form a pattern that pointed toward a previously hidden doorway. The heavy stone door slid open with a deep rumble, revealing another tunnel that descended into darkness.

"We don't stop now," Sylv said, his voice resolute. "Whatever's down there, we face it together."

Rashe, still weak but standing with Kala's support, nodded. "Lead the way. If I have to die again, I might as well make it worth something."

The companions exchanged weary smiles, their bond stronger than ever in the wake of Rashe's near-death. Together, they stepped through the doorway, leaving the chamber and its trials behind.

The new tunnel was narrower, the air growing colder with every step. The walls were lined with more glowing runes, their light flickering as if alive. The hum of the wards returned, louder and more insistent, vibrating through the stone.

Adran leaned heavily on Sylv, his strength not yet fully restored. "These runes are ancient," he said, his voice hoarse. "They're meant to test us—to see if we're worthy of the grimoire."

"Well, we've made it this far," Bevin said, his tone dry. "I'd say we're doing all right."

The path ended abruptly at a massive chasm, its depths lost in darkness. A narrow stone bridge stretched across, its surface slick with moisture. On the other side, a faint glow hinted at another chamber.

"This has trap written all over it," Morros muttered, eyeing the bridge warily.

"Agreed," Sylv said. "Bevin, can you shoot an arrow across? Let's see if anything happens."

Bevin nodded, drawing an arrow and firing it toward the far side. The moment the arrow touched the bridge, the runes flared, and ghostly figures began to rise from the chasm. Translucent and wreathed in blue light, they hovered silently, their faces obscured.

"More tests," Adran said grimly. "And these won't

be as forgiving as the statues."

Sylv stepped forward, his sword gleaming in the runic light. "Then we give them no choice but to let us pass."

The group readied themselves, their weapons drawn and their spirits bolstered by the knowledge that, even in the face of death, they could bring each other back. The grimoire awaited, its secrets drawing them deeper into the abyss—and into the heart of their greatest challenge yet.

Chapter 27

The ghostly figures rose from the chasm like a tide of malevolence, their pale blue light casting eerie shadows across the narrow stone bridge. They hovered, silent for a moment, before surging forward with a bone-chilling screech that reverberated through the cavern.

"Here they come!" Sylv shouted, raising his sword as the first wave descended upon them.

Kala met the charge head-on, his massive warhammer crashing into the spectral forms. Each strike sent shockwaves through their incorporeal bodies, but they reformed almost instantly. "They're tougher than they look!" he bellowed, swinging again with all his might.

Bevin, positioned at the rear, loosed arrows enchanted with Adran's light. Each glowing shaft pierced the ghostly cores, shattering several of the apparitions into dissipating wisps. "Aim for their hearts!" he called out. "It's their only weakness!"

Morros darted through the chaos with the precision of a blade dancer, his twin daggers flashing as he struck at the glowing cores with surgical accuracy. Despite his agility, the ghosts' sheer numbers kept him moving constantly, narrowly avoiding their claw-like hands.

Rashe stood near the center of the group, his lute in hand. As his fingers danced across the strings, a rousing melody filled the air, infusing his companions with renewed energy. "Faster, stronger, smarter!" he sang, his voice carrying above the din of battle. The music pushed their movements to the limit, turning near-misses into strikes and parries into ripostes.

Adran stood at the rear, his staff glowing with celestial light as he maintained a protective barrier around the group. The shield flickered under the relentless assault of the ghosts, but his calm voice grounded the group. "Hold your positions!" he called, his magic flaring as he sent bursts of divine energy into the fray.

The ghosts' assault grew more intense, their shrieks piercing the companions' ears as they lunged in waves. Sylv fought at the forefront, his sword a blur as he struck at the glowing cores of the specters. Each successful blow dispersed another ghost, but for every one that fell, two more seemed to take its place.

"These things don't stop!" Kala roared, smashing

another specter into the stone. Cracks spider webbed across the bridge, adding an element of danger to every swing of his hammer.

Bevin climbed onto a narrow ledge along the bridge's edge, giving him a better vantage point. His arrows flew true, each shot expertly finding its mark. "We're thinning them out!" he called, though sweat dripped down his face from the effort.

"Not fast enough," Morros muttered as he flipped over a specter, plunging his daggers into its core mid-air. He landed in a crouch, immediately rolling to avoid a ghost's swipe. "Rashe, give me something big!"

Rashe's music shifted, the tempo quickening into a frenetic rhythm. The notes seemed to crackle with energy, vibrating through the air like a living thing. The ghosts recoiled, their forms flickering under the auditory onslaught.

"Keep pushing forward!" Sylv shouted. "We need to reach solid ground!"

One by one, the companions advanced across the bridge, their movements precise and coordinated. Kala brought up the rear, his hammer clearing a path as the others reached the far side. Adran, sweat pouring from his brow, cast a final surge of light that exploded across the bridge, scattering the remaining ghosts into the abyss.

The ancient stone shuddered beneath them,

cracks widening as the bridge collapsed with a deafening roar. Dust and debris filled the air, but the companions stood safely on solid ground, their breaths ragged.

"That was too close," Rashe said, leaning heavily on his lute. "I hate ghosts. Too intangible for my taste."

"Then you'll love whatever's ahead," Sylv replied grimly, pointing to the glowing doorway at the end of the path. "No time to rest. The grimoire's close."

Beyond the doorway lay a massive circular chamber. The air was colder here, carrying the scent of decay and age. The walls were lined with towering shelves filled with crumbling tomes, each emanating a faint magical aura. At the center of the room, resting atop an ornate pedestal, was the grimoire. Its presence dominated the space, its faint glow casting long shadows across the chamber.

Before the companions could approach, a towering figure emerged from the darkness. The lich stood tall, its skeletal frame cloaked in flowing black robes that writhed like living shadows. Its eyes burned with green fire, and its bony hands clutched a staff crowned with a dark crystal that pulsed with malevolent energy.

"You dare disturb my sanctuary?" the lich intoned, its voice a chilling echo. "The grimoire belongs to me. Leave now, and I may grant you the mercy of a quick death."

Sylv stepped forward, his sword gleaming in the pale light. "We don't bargain with monsters. That grimoire doesn't belong to you, and we'll take it—whether you like it or not."

The lich let out a hollow laugh, the sound reverberating like a death knell. "Then you shall join the countless fools who came before you. None who enter this chamber leave alive."

The lich raised its staff, and darkness surged outward. Shadows coalesced into monstrous forms, each more twisted and horrifying than the last. The companions readied themselves, their weapons glowing faintly under the influence of Adran's magic.

The shadows attacked first, their movements quick and erratic. Kala charged into the fray, his hammer a beacon of destruction as he crushed the creatures with earth-shaking force. Sylv flanked him, his sword a blur of light as he cleaved through the writhing darkness.

Bevin took up position near the back, his arrows enchanted to pierce even the most ethereal forms. Each shot found its mark, scattering shadowy fragments across the chamber.

Rashe's music shifted to a defiant march, the melody weaving through the battle like a thread of hope. "Give 'em everything!" he shouted, strumming harder as the notes seemed to clash with the dark energy in the room.

Morros darted through the chaos, his daggers flashing as he struck at the shadow beasts' weak points. He moved with a dancer's grace, his strikes precise and lethal.

The lich, untouched by the initial assault, raised its staff and unleashed a wave of dark energy. The companions were thrown back, their bodies hitting the ground with bone-jarring force. Sylv recovered quickly, his eyes blazing with determination. "We need to take it down now!"

The group regrouped, their movements more coordinated as they pressed the attack. Kala and Sylv drew the lich's focus, their weapons clashing with its staff in a flurry of sparks and dark energy. Bevin provided covering fire, his arrows forcing the lich to split its attention.

Adran, despite his exhaustion, summoned a blinding surge of light that momentarily weakened the lich's defenses. "Now!" he shouted.

Rashe and Morros exchanged a glance, an unspoken understanding passing between them. Rashe's music shifted to a hauntingly powerful melody, each note vibrating with raw energy. The sound seemed to disrupt the lich's magic, its dark aura flickering as the music crescendoed.

"Go!" Rashe shouted, his fingers a blur on the

lute strings.

Morros moved like a shadow, his daggers gleaming in the light of Rashe's song. He darted past the lich's defenses, his movements too quick for the creature to counter. With a final leap, he plunged both daggers into the lich's chest, striking its glowing core.

The lich let out an ear-shattering scream as cracks spread through its skeletal frame. The green fire in its eyes flared one last time before extinguishing, and its body collapsed into ash. The room fell silent, the oppressive energy lifting as the grimoire's glow steadied.

The companions stood in silence, their breaths heavy as they stared at the grimoire. Its faint light pulsed gently, a stark contrast to the chaos that had just unfolded.

Sylv approached the pedestal, his hand hovering over the ancient book. "We've earned this," he said quietly. "But the cost was almost too high."

Adran knelt beside Morros, who leaned heavily on the assassin. "You good?" the healer asked, exhaustion clear in his voice.

Morros smirked weakly. "I've had worse," he said, though his pale face told a different story.

Rashe collapsed onto a nearby stone, his lute clutched tightly. "We actually did it," he said, his voice trembling with relief. "I think I need a drink.

Or several."

Sylv carefully lifted the grimoire, its weight surprising despite its size. "This isn't just a victory," he said, turning to the group. "This is a responsibility. Whatever power this holds, we'll make sure it's used to protect—not destroy."

As they prepared to leave, Rashe and Morros exchanged a grin. "Not bad for a bard and an assassin," Rashe said.

"Not bad at all," Morros replied, his voice steady despite his fatigue.

Together, the Fortuitous Few turned and stepped out of the chamber, the grimoire in hand and their bond stronger than ever. The road ahead was uncertain, but for the first time in what felt like ages, they walked with the confidence of those who had faced death—and won.

Chapter 28

The Fortuitous Few emerged from the cavern, the golden light of late afternoon spilling over the jagged hills of Lacronshire. The fresh air, cool and crisp, was a stark contrast to the oppressive atmosphere of the chambers they had left behind. Each of them bore marks of the trials they had faced—cuts, bruises, exhaustion—but there was a quiet pride in their steps as they carried the grimoire out of its ancient prison.

Sylv led the group, the grimoire tucked safely in a reinforced satchel slung across his back. It emanated a faint warmth, as if alive, a constant reminder of the power they now carried. Behind him, Kala shouldered his hammer with a grunt, while Bevin scanned the horizon, his sharp eyes ever alert for threats. Rashe and Morros walked side by side, their banter lighthearted despite the weariness in their voices, and Adran followed close, his staff glowing faintly as he leaned on it for support.

"Do we have to walk the whole way back?" Rashe groaned, kicking at a loose stone on the path. "We've defeated ghosts, liches, and gods know what else. Haven't we earned a shortcut?"

"I doubt the grimoire comes with a teleportation spell," Sylv replied dryly, adjusting the satchel. "And even if it did, I'm not sure I'd trust it."

"We'll make camp soon," Adran said. "We need rest before nightfall."

By twilight, they had found a suitable spot to camp—a sheltered hollow beneath a rocky over-hang, with a small stream nearby. Kala and Sylv worked together to build a fire, its warm light pushing back the growing darkness. Bevin set up a perimeter of simple tripwires, each strung with small bells that would sound at the slightest disturbance.

As they settled in, Rashe strummed a soft, sooth-ing melody on his lute while Adran passed out rations. The meal was simple—dried meat, bread, and a few roasted roots from a nearby patch of wild carrots—but it filled their bellies and bolstered their spirits.

"Who's taking first watch?" Sylv asked as he leaned back against a log.

"I will," Kala volunteered, his voice gruff but steady. "I can't sleep yet, anyway."

The others nodded, one by one slipping into their

bedrolls as the fire crackled softly. Kala stood, his hammer resting against a nearby rock, and took up his position on a flat outcrop overlooking the camp.

The first few hours of Kala's watch were uneventful, the quiet night broken only by the occasional rustle of leaves or distant call of an owl. But as the moon rose higher, a faint sound caught his attention—a low whispering, like wind through the trees.

Kala stood, his eyes narrowing as he scanned the darkness. The whispering grew louder, though no wind stirred the leaves. Slowly, he approached the edge of the camp, his hammer at the ready.

"Who's there?" he growled.

The whispering stopped abruptly, leaving an eerie silence in its wake. Kala's grip on his hammer tightened, but after a moment, he stepped back to the fire. "Must've been my imagination," he muttered, though his eyes remained on the treeline for the rest of his watch.

When Kala woke Bevin for the second watch, the ranger stretched, rubbing his eyes before taking his place near the fire. The night was colder now, and he pulled his cloak tighter as he settled in.

An hour passed quietly, and Bevin began to relax, his sharp eyes scanning the horizon out of habit. Suddenly, a loud *thud* startled him, followed by a string of colorful curses in a deep, gravelly voice.

Bevin turned, his hand going to his bow. To his utter astonishment, a dwarf lay sprawled in the middle of the camp, as if he had fallen from the sky. The stout figure, dressed in patched leather and carrying an enormous pack, scrambled to his feet, brushing off dirt and leaves.

"By the gods, where in the blasted hells am I now?" the dwarf muttered, glancing around. His eyes landed on Bevin, and he gave a curt nod. "You didn't see that."

Before Bevin could respond, the dwarf hoisted his pack and marched off into the darkness, muttering to himself. Bevin sat frozen for a moment, then chuckled softly. "I'm not even going to try to explain that."

Rashe took the third watch, sitting cross-legged by the fire with his lute resting on his lap. The night was still, and he idly plucked at the strings, letting the quiet melody keep him company.

As the firelight dimmed, small orbs of light began to appear in the distance. They hovered just beyond the treeline, swaying gently as if caught in an invisible current. Rashe watched them with a mix of curiosity and unease.

"Fairies? Spirits? Or am I just too tired to think straight?" he murmured.

The lights flickered, then faded one by one,

leaving the forest in darkness. Rashe shook his head, strumming a lively tune to chase away the lingering chill. "If they wanted trouble, they'd have found it," he said to himself, his voice calm but firm.

Adran took the final watch, his staff glowing softly as he walked the perimeter of the camp. The night was quiet, the stars bright overhead. But as he approached the edge of the hollow, he felt a sudden presence—an invisible weight in the air that made the hairs on his neck stand up.

"Show yourself," he said, his voice steady despite the unease creeping over him.

A figure emerged from the shadows—a tall, humanoid shape cloaked in flowing black robes. Its face was obscured, and it carried no weapons, but its mere presence exuded an aura of ancient power.

"You carry the grimoire," the figure said, its voice like wind through dry leaves. "Do you know what you hold?"

Adran tightened his grip on his staff. "Enough to know it's dangerous."

The figure tilted its head, as if studying him. "Be cautious, healer. Power such as that demands a heavy price."

Before Adran could respond, the figure dissolved into the night, leaving only the faint scent of earth and decay. Adran returned to the fire, his expression thoughtful as he watched the first rays of dawn creep over the horizon.

The morning sun hung low in the sky as the Fortuitous Few made their way through a narrow valley flanked by steep, jagged cliffs. Shadows stretched long across the dirt road, the air thick with an uneasy silence. Birds that had been chirping moments before fell eerily quiet, and even the wind seemed to hold its breath.

Bevin halted abruptly, raising a hand to signal the others. "Hold up," he said, his voice barely above a whisper. His sharp eyes scanned the rocky terrain ahead. "Something's not right."

Before anyone could respond, a low, mournful wail echoed through the valley, sending a shiver down their spines. The sound seemed to come from everywhere and nowhere all at once, resonating in the pit of their stomachs like a funeral dirge.

"What in the gods' name was that?" Rashe muttered, tightening his grip on his lute.

From the shadows ahead, the faint clatter of hooves began to rise, like distant thunder rolling closer. Shapes emerged from the gloom—dark, skeletal forms astride equally macabre mounts. The undead riders came into view, their armor rusted and broken, their weapons jagged and cruel. Their mounts were skeletal warhorses, their eyes glowing with unholy fire, their mouths frozen in macabre grins that seemed to mock the living.

At their head rode a towering figure, a skeletal knight encased in decayed plate armor. His rusted greatsword gleamed dully in the pale light, and his hollow, glowing eyes fixed on the companions.

"Sinners and defilers," the knight intoned, his voice a hollow rasp that carried unnaturally through the valley. "Surrender the grimoire, and I may grant you an end free of suffering. Resist, and you will join my ranks for eternity."

Sylv stepped forward, his sword already drawn, the sunlight catching the polished blade. "We don't surrender to monsters," he said coldly. "If you want it, you'll have to take it."

The knight's skeletal grin widened. "So be it."

With a ghastly screech, the knight raised his greatsword and pointed it toward the companions. The riders surged forward, their mounts thundering down the road with unnatural speed. The sound of their charge was deafening—bone grinding against bone, hooves pounding like drums of war, and the echoing howls of undead malice.

Kala charged to the front, planting himself like an immovable wall. "With me!" he bellowed, his warhammer swinging in a wide arc. The first rider to reach him raised its jagged scimitar, but Kala's hammer struck first, shattering the skeleton's ribcage and sending its bones scattering across the road.

Sylv flanked Kala, his blade flashing as he parried a lance aimed for his chest. With a precise counterstrike, he severed the undead rider's arm at the shoulder, sending its weapon clattering to the ground. The skeletal mount reared, but Sylv drove his blade into its skull, reducing it to a pile of lifeless bones.

Bevin, positioned at the rear, loosed arrow after arrow, his shots piercing through rusted armor and striking true. "They're fast, but not invincible!" he called, drawing another arrow and taking aim at a rider bearing down on Adran.

The arrow struck the rider's spine, shattering its connection to the saddle. The skeletal warrior crumbled to the ground, its mount veering off wildly before collapsing in a heap.

The undead riders were relentless, their numbers greater than they had initially appeared. For every skeleton struck down, another seemed to rise from the swirling dust. Rashe stood near the center of the group, his lute ringing out a fierce battle anthem. The notes surged through the air, quickening his companions' movements and dulling the chill of fear that crept into their hearts.

Morros darted through the chaos like a shadow, his daggers finding gaps in the undead warriors' armor with unerring precision. He vaulted onto the back of a skeletal horse, driving both blades into the rider's neck before leaping off as the creature collapsed in a heap of bones.

"Nice trick," Rashe called, strumming a triumphant chord.

"Stay alive, and I'll teach you," Morros quipped, disappearing into the fray once more.

Kala roared as he struck another rider, the impact of his hammer sending cracks rippling through the ground. "Adran! Some of these bastards aren't staying down!"

Adran, standing slightly back from the melee, raised his staff high. A burst of radiant light exploded outward, washing over the battlefield. Several of the undead riders screeched as the holy energy burned through their corrupted forms, reducing them to ash. The others faltered for a moment, their movements sluggish.

"Now's your chance!" Adran shouted.

Sylv took the opportunity, charging the skeletal knight who led the attack. Their blades clashed with a deafening ring, sparks flying as steel met rusted iron. The knight's strength was unnatural, each strike forcing Sylv to dig his heels into the dirt to hold his ground.

"You cannot win," the knight rasped, his glowing eyes burning brighter. "This road is your grave."

"Not today," Sylv growled, sidestepping a brutal overhead swing. He countered with a strike aimed at the knight's exposed ribs, his blade slicing cleanly through the brittle bone.

The skeletal knight reeled, but he was far from defeated. Raising his greatsword high, he bellowed an incantation in a language older than the stones beneath their feet. The ground shook, and dark tendrils of energy erupted from the earth, lashing out at the companions.

One of the tendrils struck Bevin, knocking him to the ground. His bow skittered out of reach as he struggled to rise, the corrupted energy sapping his strength.

"Hold on!" Rashe called, his music shifting to a protective tune. The notes formed a shimmering barrier around Bevin, deflecting the tendrils long enough for him to grab his bow and roll out of harm's way.

Kala charged the knight, his hammer raised high. The lich-like warrior turned to meet him, their weapons clashing in a burst of sparks. "Stay down, you pile of bones!" Kala roared, swinging with enough force to knock the knight off his mount.

The skeletal knight crashed to the ground, but even dismounted, he fought with unholy ferocity. He swung his greatsword in a wide arc, forcing Kala and Sylv to step back.

Morros took advantage of the opening. Slipping behind the knight, he drove both daggers into the creature's exposed spine, twisting them for maximum effect. The knight howled, his glowing eyes flickering as cracks spread across his armor.

"Finish it!" Sylv shouted, stepping forward to deliver the final blow. With a powerful strike, he brought his sword down on the knight's skull, splitting it cleanly in two. The undead leader collapsed into a pile of lifeless bones, and the remaining riders faltered, their connection to the dark magic severed.

One by one, the skeletal warriors crumbled, their mounts dissolving into dust. The valley fell silent once more, save for the companions' ragged breaths.

As the dust settled, they noticed several skeletal horses standing motionless, their fiery eyes dimmed but still glowing faintly. Unlike their fallen riders, these mounts had not been destroyed.

"Think they're safe to ride?" Rashe asked, eyeing the creatures warily.

Kala approached one of the horses, placing a cautious hand on its bony neck. The creature snorted softly but didn't recoil. "Seems tame enough," he said with a shrug.

The companions each claimed a mount, climbing onto the skeletal steeds. The creatures moved smoothly, their hooves making barely a sound as they began the ride back to Cavranosk.

"Creepy, but practical," Bevin remarked, adjusting his position in the saddle.

Sylv glanced back at the group, his face grim but satisfied. "We've earned this shortcut. Let's get back to the village—and hope there are no more surprises waiting for us."

With that, they rode into the fading light, the grimoire secure and their spirits lifted, ready to deliver their prize and face whatever came next.

Chapter 29

The Fortuitous Few entered the hamlet of Cavranosk as the sun dipped below the horizon, painting the sky with hues of orange and pink. Their skeletal steeds carried them silently through the cobbled streets, the eerie clatter of bone hooves on stone drawing wary glances from the villagers. At first, gasps of fear rippled through the crowd as they beheld the undead mounts. But then recognition dawned, and the initial alarm transformed into cheers of celebration. The villagers surged forward to greet their saviors, their faces alight with gratitude and awe.

Sylv dismounted first, his steps deliberate as he approached the elder, who stood waiting in the village square. The elder's staff glimmered faintly in the gathering twilight, and his eyes gleamed with a mixture of relief and reverence. The grimoire, still secure in Sylv's satchel, pulsed with a faint, rhythmic warmth, as if it were a living thing.

"You have returned," the elder said, his voice

heavy with emotion. "The grimoire is safe. And with it, the heart of Cavranosk. You have done what we could never dream of achieving."

Sylv unslung the satchel and handed it to the elder with both hands, his expression solemn. "It wasn't just for you," he said. "This power is too great to leave unguarded. We retrieved it to ensure it would not fall into the wrong hands."

The elder cradled the book as though it were a child, the light of his staff intensifying in its presence. "You speak wisely, Sylv. But this grimoire is not merely a tool of destruction. It carries the potential to strengthen and protect. You've risked your lives to reclaim it, and it is only right that it repays you in kind."

The elder gestured for the companions to follow him into the village hall, a modest stone building that now seemed to hum with energy in the presence of the ancient artifact. Inside, he placed the grimoire on an intricately carved pedestal at the center of the room. The book's glow intensified, casting the chamber in an otherworldly light.

"You have proven yourselves worthy not only of this village's gratitude but also of its greatest treasure," the elder said. "Let the grimoire honor your courage."

With a slow, deliberate motion, the elder opened the book. Its pages turned on their own, the ancient script shimmering as it settled on a passage that seemed to leap out in waves of light. He began to chant in a language none of them understood, his voice resonating with a deep, melodic power.

The room grew warmer, and the companions felt a strange tingling sensation coursing through their bodies. Beams of light emanated from the grimoire, connecting with each of them in turn. The energy was not overwhelming, but invigorating, filling them with a sense of clarity and strength they had never known.

Sylv felt the light settle over his heart, a steady pulse that seemed to synchronize with his own. His mind sharpened, the countless battles and strategies he had encountered throughout his life crystallizing into perfect clarity. He could feel his muscles strengthen and his reflexes quicken, but more importantly, a newfound sense of leadership and connection to his companions blossomed within him.

"You have the heart of a protector," the elder said to him. "Now, you will always know the path to safeguard those who depend on you."

For Kala, the light was a warm, encompassing weight, like the embrace of an old friend. It coursed through his arms and shoulders, hardening his already formidable muscles into something almost unyielding. But it also touched his mind, granting him the wisdom to temper his strength with precision.

"You are the wall upon which chaos breaks," the elder intoned. "May you wield your power with purpose and restraint."

Bevin felt the light settle over his eyes and hands, an electric surge of precision that made the world seem sharper, more vivid. Every detail of the room seemed to stand out—the grain of the wooden beams, the faint quiver of the elder's staff. He tested his bowstring, and it hummed with a resonance he had never felt before.

"You are the watchman, the harbinger of justice," the elder said. "Let no threat escape your sight."

For Adran, the light was a soothing balm, flowing into his hands and chest with an almost over-whelming warmth. His connection to the celestial forces he served deepened, the divine power within him expanding like a roaring fire. He felt a new understanding of healing and protection unfurl in his mind.

"You are the light in the darkest moments," the elder said. "Let your hands mend not only the body but also the spirit."

Morros stood still as the light wrapped around him, cool and silent, like the caress of a shadow. His movements felt lighter, faster, and the daggers at his side seemed to hum with anticipation. The power also touched his instincts, sharpening them until he felt he could predict an enemy's movements before they even began.

"You are the unseen, the dagger in the night," the elder said. "Your silence will be your strength."

For Rashe, the light resonated with his music, each note of his lute seeming to come alive with a brilliance that set the air vibrating. His voice, when he tested it, was richer, more commanding, as though it could weave spells as easily as melodies.

"You are the voice of unity," the elder said. "May your songs inspire the hearts of heroes and terrify the hearts of your enemies."

When the light finally receded, the room returned to stillness. The companions exchanged glances, each of them feeling the change within. They were stronger, faster, more attuned to their abilities than ever before.

The elder closed the grimoire, his face weary but content. "You are no longer simply travelers," he said. "You are champions. And Cavranosk will always remember you as such."

The group left the hall to a village waiting eagerly outside. Word had already spread of their enhanced abilities, and the celebration that followed was unlike anything they had seen before. A grand feast was held, with music, dancing, and laughter filling the square late into the night.

Over the next week, the companions embraced the rare opportunity for respite. Each of them pursued their own path of renewal, bonding with the villagers and each other. Kala and Bevin worked with the hunters and smiths to refine their skills, while Adran trained the village healers in the advanced techniques he had learned from the grimoire. Sylv spent long hours with the elder, strategizing ways to safeguard the village's future. Morros and Rashe, meanwhile, became beloved figures among the children, entertaining them with tales and tricks.

The week passed quickly, but it left a lasting mark on both the village and the Fortuitous Few. Cavranosk would never again be a simple hamlet, and the companions would carry the lessons and connections they had forged here into the battles to come.

On the morning of their departure, the villagers gathered in the square to see them off. The undead steeds, standing obediently at the edge of the square, had been outfitted with sturdy saddles and supplies for the journey ahead. Despite their eerie appearance, the horses had proven loyal and tireless.

The elder approached Sylv one last time, his staff glowing faintly. "The road before you is long, but you will not walk alone. Cavranosk is with you, always."

Sylv nodded, his expression was serious but grateful. "We'll come back. Not for the grimoire, but to see what you've built."

With a final round of farewells, the Fortuitous Few mounted their skeletal horses and rode out of Cavranosk. The villagers' cheers followed them into the hills, a reminder of the lives they had touched and the hope they had restored.

As they rode toward the distant airship, the companions felt a renewed sense of purpose. They were no longer merely adventurers. They were protectors, leaders, and symbols of resilience in a world that desperately needed them. And together, they would face whatever challenges lay ahead— unbroken, unyielding, and unstoppable.